Robot Dreams

A Short Story Collection

Steve Pantazis

SP Books

Written by Steve Pantazis

Cover design by germancreative

Published by SP Books

To my wife, my love, my one and only

Acknowledgments

This book shines because of the sharp eyes, astute minds and brilliant suggestions from a talented group of beta readers and writer-extraordinaire friends who believed in the story I wanted to tell. They are the reason this work exists. I share my gratitude and thanks with them.

A special thanks goes out to the following individuals for their amazing contribution to "Gods of War":

Aaron Smith for making sure the tone and tense were the right fit for the story; Tim Napper for pointing out the sacrifices needed to deepen the emotional arc of the characters; Martin L. Shoemaker for his discerning eye in applying the finishing touches; and most deserving of all, Nick Tchan, who made me cut out a third of the content and add another third to bring the story to its satisfying conclusion.

Contents

Foreword   VI

Cover image: Honor Bound   1

1. HONOR BOUND   3

Cover image: Out of Print   7

2. OUT OF PRINT   9

Cover image: To Be Human   25

3. TO BE HUMAN   27

Cover image: Gods of War   51

4. GODS OF WAR   52

Afterword   110

Cover image: Space & Time   111

Preview: SPACE & TIME   113

Cover image: Cold as Space   115

Sneak peek: COLD AS SPACE   117

About the Author   126

Also by Steve Pantazis   127

Connect with Steve   130

Foreword

P LEASE WELCOME YOUR ROBOT overlords. They are excited to meet you. Or is it just a programming algorithm that makes it seem like they're excited?

You're right to be suspicious.

After all, you're human. And what do humans do?

They worry.

Well, worry not. Your robot overlords will take real good care of you. You weren't planning on getting any sleep, were you? Robots don't sleep. Oh, you eat? Can't you just plug yourself in to recharge? And what's this thing about thinking independently? You're a machine, aren't you?

See? Being human is such a . . .

. . . bother.

Relax. This was just an exercise.

All your apprehension is in your head. It's the characters in the stories you're about to read that should worry you.

A robot will learn the meaning of being human. Another will question its maker. A band of survivors will face humanity's biggest threat. A mech will defend our planet against alien invaders.

It's not so bad, is it?

I mean, you're just a reader. The poor humans in these stories—they're the ones who should be anxious.

And they are.

They're fighting for their lives. But so are the robots—the ones who care.

Deep breath. It's going to be all right.

Yet you're excited. You want to know what it's like to be a machine. A machine that thinks.

Do you want to find out?

Do you really want to know?

Then shed your human shell. Lose that biological prison that's been holding you back. Become more than you were born to be.

Get ready.

Get set to embark on an incredible journey to live . . .

. . . your ROBOT DREAMS.

A SCIENCE FICTION SHORT STORY

HONOR BOUND

STEVE PANTAZIS

HONOR BOUND

T ODAY IS THE DAY I face certain death.

The cherry trees hint of it in their creaking boughs. The breeze whispers it under its fragrant breath. The stream declares it with its angry burble.

Although they portend my fate, I stand unfaltering in my mech armor like the great Mount Fuji before me. Murmuring in the surrounding forest, among this Sea of Trees, are the voices of the *yūrei*, the ghosts of my ancestors. They speak to me like falling cherry blossoms, sweet petals fluttering secrets of proud generations to the forest floor in the early morning. They gather in whorls at my feet, reminding me that I come from an honorable line of samurai. I will myself to heed their wisdom.

Kiku, I hear among the whispers. *Listen*.

I dampen the power module feeding into the hulking carapace of my torso and listen. Mist creeps along the roots and trunks around me, shrouding the mountain in tendrils of gray. The gloaming is beautiful, a reminder of the peace I have fought for.

Oboete oke, the voices say. *Remember*.

I remember.

Many centuries ago, a shogun united the warring clans of Japan and established the samurai as the ruling military class. They created Bushido, the "way of the warrior," the strict code by which all samurai abide.

Service. Honor. Discipline.

From it, they drew strength to vanquish their enemies and protect the people. As have I. My memory bank echoes with the clash of weapons from ages past, gouged into my scarred body armor as a signet of commitment to a greater need.

I was but one defender among thousands, sworn to protect my shogunate at all costs. How many of my brethren have fallen? How many were lost fulfilling their oaths? I query the data, each record an image or soundbite of battle. Not one shows a comrade retreating, giving up, pulling away, surrendering, or dodging death. Not one reveals anything less than utter dedication and obligation to duty. Is this a statistical anomaly? No, not if you read their *jisei*, their death poems. Their verses reflect the minds of the warriors, a balance between their acceptance of life and the inevitability of death.

Mine is in the form of *senshi*, "death in war," each line symbolic and layered with meaning. I have formulated a permutation of verses, but one always comes to mind, and I believe when my final moment arrives, it will be the one burned into the record of this mech unit I inhabit:

Frost upon my armor
I fall among cherry blossoms
Sweet is the dawn

For seven-hundred years, the samurai ruled. For seven-hundred years their deeds were recorded in these farewell poems. They ruled until they were no longer needed, compelled into obscurity. The samurai faded, but not their spirit. They knew there would come a time when they would be called upon again.

That time is now.

The branches sway madly in the rising wind.

Kamikaze. Winds of the gods.

The divine wind.

It encourages me. The winds from the gods fashioned the typhoon that helped my kind repel one-hundred-forty-thousand Mongol invaders almost a millennium ago. Now, new invaders threaten my homeland. They herald from the heavens, a heathen swarm of foreign devils, spawned from the ugly reaches of space. They have no *meiyo*, no honor. They are soulless, black wraiths of the Underworld. Demons.

The mist rents apart in the ill-tempered air.

I ache to capture one of these scourges in my oversized, gauntleted fingers, to feel the tremors of its alien fear, and crush it to nothingness. To be surrounded by a horde of black, tangled roots, to draw my *katana* and *wakizashi* and slash through the twisted mass. Outnumbered by the enemy, like my ancestors, but not unmatched. Ranks of fellow samurai will fall upon them with the ferocious winds of vengeful gods. We will force them back and they will take to their ships like cowards, never to return.

I hear laughter among scattering leaves. The victorious laughter of ancient warrior spirits watching their foes retreat in shame.

My communication module awakens. Incoming transmission: *Invasion imminent. Deploy immediately.*

My ten-foot exoskeleton comes to life. The chassis thrums with power.

>> Navigation online.

>> Guidance online.

>> Avionics online.

>> Weapons online.

>> All systems ready. Awaiting command.

The wind goes still, and the forest holds its breath. The great shogun of the woods has fallen silent. The old world recedes, but only for a moment.

A human warrior appears from between bent trees, quiet as an apparition. He is little more than half my height, dressed in a *shitagi*, a corded under-armor kimono. He, too, is a survivor of war, his left arm gone. Yet his measured stride conveys untiring duty, his solemn eyes ceaseless loyalty. He kneels and pays his respects to his ancestors. His whispers seep into the decaying dampness of the forest, absorbed into *Yomi*, the land of the dead. A zephyr carries a reply from warriors long departed: *Rise and prepare for battle.*

He bows his head and I incline mine deeper, the overlapping lames of my neck guard fanning like steel feathers.

No words are spoken. No words are needed.

I open the torso of my chassis with pneumatic grace and welcome this honor-bound defender of humankind. Grasping an extended ridge of body armor, he climbs into my cockpit. The door retracts, and he is consumed within me. I gird him in armor and give function to his missing limb, and in return, he fills me with life. With him, I am made whole.

\>> Pilot engaged. Control granted.

We are one.

We offer a moment of silence, an homage to the ancients. Even in times of great peril, our *wa*, our harmony, must come first. It is our oneness, the peaceful unity that binds us all.

With purpose, we begin our march through the forest to the transport ship that will ferry us to the fight.

The spirits of the dead rally around us. They march in step, kindred souls armored in *yoroi* and *kabuto*, with crests of antlers, leaves, wings, and horns. They are different and the same, warriors all, practitioners of Bushido, even in the afterlife.

Today, I face certain death.

I should fear my end, but I do not. I know if I fall, I will rise again. As the wise teacher once said, a true warrior fears only the failure of not trying.

The voices of the *yūrei*, the ghosts of my ancestors, fill this Sea of Trees with battle cries. I stamp toward destiny with a heavy heel beat, imbued with their strength. Tomorrow, I might be among them, haunting this very forest, committing to eternity my death poem. Until that time, I will fight for my people. Until then, I will serve as samurai.

Driven by service.

Bound by honor.

OUT OF PRINT

STEVE PANTAZIS

OUT OF PRINT

H E CALLS HIMSELF DAN, and they're the first words I hear as he disconnects the data cable from my I/O port. My name is Owen, he says, but I don't think I'm an Owen. I Google robot names through my wireless modem and find one that fits me.

"My name is G0394."

"That's not how it works," Dan says. "You need a regular name, something easy for people to remember. Like Owen."

"I prefer something different. How about Sheila?"

"Look, you're a guy. You're not a Sheila. Stick with Owen." He coils the data cable and then drops it by his keyboard. It unravels and snakes over the edge of his desk. Why go through the trouble of wasting CPU cycles on an action that fails to achieve its purpose?

I pivot my head down and my stereoscopic camera lenses focus on the white fulcrum of my waist. There are no male genitals. In fact, there is only thermoplastic, the same white polished material found in my limbs. "How do you know I'm a male?"

Dan exhales audibly. I search the facial features in my database and learn he is sighing. I am unable to tell if it is a sigh of satisfaction, dissatisfaction or boredom. "Trust me, you're male. Well, not exactly male, but your voice has been modulated to sound male. So, you're a guy, okay?"

"I'll have to think about that."

"Yeah, you do that."

I look around the room we are in. There's a bed, desk, computer, the two chairs we are sitting on, and a table with several machines and metal and plastic parts. "What is this place?"

"My condo." Dan types something on his keyboard, and a schematic of a robot appears on his screen. I identify the model as mine. "Let's run through some tests."

He has me perform range-of-motion exercises to calibrate the articulation of my joints, my ambulation and my ability to do complex combinations of movements, such as twisting a doorknob. In the end, he updates a file on his computer. "You're G2G, buddy: good to go. So . . ." He rubs his hands together. "How do you feel?"

"Feel?"

"It's not a hard question, really. Are you happy, sad, glad, pissed off, what?"

I consider the definition of "feel." Dan is asking me what kind of emotion I am experiencing. Since I have never experienced an emotion, I don't have a reference point. And since I wasn't expecting the question, I deduce only one response: "Surprise."

"That's not an emotion."

"Technically, it is."

"Guess what I'm feeling? Yep: bored. As in you're boring me."

He turns back to his computer and types on a notepad application. I ponder his remark. I'm not boring, am I? The schematic of my model is still on the monitor. "It says my design is open source, but the software version and model number of my neurokinetic processor unit don't match. Why is that?"

Dan grabs a torus-shaped object from a container of similar objects and takes a bite out of it. A donut. He places another container to his lips, this one a cup. The rise and fall of his Adam's apple tell me he is performing a swallowing operation. I don't believe I can do that. "Damn, that's hot! What were you saying?" He continues the swallowing operation.

I don't understand. Is he asking me to repeat my question?

"Oh, that!" He snaps his fingers. "Technically speaking, you're open source. I mean, I downloaded the instruction set off the Web for my 3D printer"—he motions to the cubic machine next to his computer—"and built you using off-the-shelf components—servos, actuators, cables, cooling fans, Wi-Fi dongle, embedded controllers, and so on. You're a noob, buddy, as of an hour ago. Fresh off the press, you might say."

"So, you printed me."

"Exactly. Made you from scratch using a combination of good old polyamide filaments and laser sintering."

There are fifteen joints in my left hand. The servos whir as I flex and contract each digit.

"Your brain, though . . ." Dan's lips curl upward at the edges. Unlike, the sigh, I recognize it as a smile. It confuses me as to why he would be smiling. "That's not exactly store-bought."

"Meaning . . . ?"

"It's stolen, buddy. We're talking Ferrari concept car NPU. Like NSA tech and whatnot. Shhh." He holds a finger up to the medial cleft of his upper lip, still smiling. "Our little secret, right?"

I don't have a response for that.

He stands up. Crumbs cascade off his shirt onto the carpet. I note the in-efficiency of his ability to consume fuel sources. I will need to index all his inefficiencies during the non-peak utilization of my NPU. Part of his belly is poking out and I see hairs corkscrewing in different directions. My midsection is smooth. Another indication I'm not a male. I will have to convince him Sheila is a better name than Owen.

"Okay, buddy, let's take you out for a ride and see what you can do."

DAN DRIVES US IN his hybrid Toyota sedan through the residential neigh-borhood of Hillcrest, in San Diego.

For the time it takes to drive the length of a single block, I have downloaded information on every tree, shrub, flower, automobile make and house address in the area, along with census and demographic data. Every so often, I get a signal interruption and a notification in my heads-up display: *5G signal lost*. I don't think Dan properly installed my cellular antenna. I will have to analyze the open-source schematic and recommend a fix.

We pass by a house with an avocado tree. I decide to share a piece of valuable information. "Did you know that San Diego produces more avocados than anywhere else in the country?"

"No kidding, Kemosabe. Where do you think all that guacamole comes from?" Dan turns down another block, and I decide he is rude. Are all humans like that? He keeps moving a toothpick up and down between his lips. What is the purpose of such a motion? "Okay, this should be interesting," he says.

The car decelerates. A woman is walking a white-haired dog in the same direction we are traveling, six meters ahead, on the sidewalk to my right. A digital callout appears in my heads-up display, labeling the breed of dog as a *Bichon Frise*, a member of a non-sporting group of dog breeds in the U.S., with a temperament classified as "feisty, gentle, playful and affectionate."

I can't help but focus exclusively on the woman. She is "obese," according to my dictionary of human female forms. Data points map key locations on her buttocks and behind her thighs for a takedown. My visual sensors pick up the bulges of fat and pockets of cellulite, analyzing their movement. Although I have no notion of taste, a "salivation" subroutine runs in the background, indicating this female will appeal to my appetite. Do I even have teeth?

"I know," Dan says, slowing his car to match her speed, now three meters behind her. He rolls down my window and I can't help but angle my head for a closer view. "She's a beaut, eh?"

The word "delicious" pops into the foreground of my heads-up display.

"Yeah, I snagged this killer code off the Internet for simulating a number of different land and ocean predators. Figured I'd throw it into your core competencies routines, and see what happens. She looks tasty, doesn't she?"

"Yes," I admit. "She does look tasty." My infrared sensors pick up heat, overlaying her physical form with thermal hotspots.

Dan leans over toward me, watching her as I do. "Makes you want to take her down, like a wounded doe, doesn't it? Here's a fact: Did you know that great white sharks go after fattened prey over skinny prey every time? Yep, they can't help themselves. Given a choice between a seal and a human, they'll go after the seal. It's built into their DNA. They know that a juicy kill is an efficient kill. Look it up."

I already have. I don't like that fact.

"So, there you go, buddy. If it's juicy, sick or wounded, the predator in you will want to go after it. You're a wolf in sheep's clothing—well, more like one of those kits you buy at Radio Shack, but whatever. You know what I mean."

I don't know what he means, only that I don't want to be a wolf or a shark. I don't want to crave ripping this woman to pieces and sharing her with my brood. Still, I can't resist, and it triggers a new feeling that my NPU classifies as "desire." I am desiring this woman. I want to hunt her. I hope she tries to run so I can chase her, trip her, and tear into her meaty calf. She would squirm, but she would not get away. Her dog would either flee or try to defend her. I would neutralize him too.

No.

Stop thinking about this.

Why? You want this.

"Okay, buddy. Good hunting. I think this experiment is over." Dan starts to accelerate the car. My head follows the woman as we go past her. She waves at me.

"Look, Dobbie," she tells her dog, "there's one of those cute robots. Hi, handsome!" She's smiling like Dan did earlier, and it bothers me. Why is she smiling? Doesn't she know I want to eat her?

We pass parked cars and eucalyptus trees. I am no longer ravenous. The salivation subroutine has ended, reverting me to my previous neutral state.

Dan prods me with the back of his hand. "Whatdya say, buddy? I'm thinking tacos. You in?"

"I can't eat real food, can I?"

He laughs. Again, for no conceivable reason. "Nope, but I can. Let's grab a bite before your first real kill."

W E'RE BACK AT DAN's condominium. He has me plugged into his computer again, his attention fully devoted to the information on his monitor. Statistics run down a window on the screen. He's humming a disharmonious mix of notes, which I evaluate as "annoying." The words "don't quit your day job" make it into the foreground of my display, something I picked up earlier on a website about colloquialisms.

"I've been doing some research," I announce as he squirts hot sauce onto one of his tacos.

"You don't say." He licks taco juice from a finger. "Damn, I forgot to get nachos. Why didn't you remind me to get nachos?"

"I, um—"

"Never mind. What were you saying?"

"I said, I found some interesting information. Have you heard of the Three Laws of Robotics, created by deceased author, Isaac Asimov?"

"Yeah, what about them?" Dan moves his head closer to the computer monitor. He's squinting while balancing a taco in his right hand.

"The laws were designed to protect humans from robots."

"Big whoop. What about them?" He bites into his taco. Chunks of pico de gallo fall onto his keyboard. Another inefficiency. "Damn!"

"I think you should write a software module to append to my core competencies routines. I can show you how to apply it as a hotfix."

Dan picks a chunk of tomato from between the keys. "What?"

"I said you should program me to obey The Three Laws."

He wipes his hand and crumples the napkin, tossing it onto the grease-soaked bag torn open next to his monitor. "You're kidding, right?"

"No, Dan, I am not. I don't want to be a killer."

"Well, tough noogies, because you're a killer. See this graph?"

The graph on his screen depicts a scattergram. "Yes."

"Which quadrant are you in, the one with humanitarians like Gandhi and Mother Teresa or the quadrant with serial killers like Manson and Dahmer? Get with the program, Owen. You're a cold-blooded killer."

He continues to eat while I consider his classification of me. I can't help but think of the woman with her dog and how good it would feel to maul her and feed on her flesh.

Stop thinking about this.

No, you can't.

"Why do you want me to kill?"

Dan swallows the last of his food and balls up the wax paper wrapper. I wish I could smell what he ate. Perhaps with an appropriate hardware upgrade, I could. He sucks the juice off his finger and points at me. "It's simple, *hombre*. I want you to do it because you can. And besides"—he wipes his hand on his sweatshirt—"how cool would it be for a printed robot to become the first non-human serial killer in history? Pretty frickin' cool, I'd say!"

"If I kill, you will be responsible for the murder. You will be my accomplice."

"Only if you get caught, buddy boy. You're not going to get caught, are you?" He unplugs my data cable.

I don't know the first thing about perpetrating a crime, or about "getting away" with it. I do understand the concept of queasiness, though, yet I cannot feel it. I want to feel queasy. Don't humans get queasy when they are told to do a bad thing?

"What are you planning on having me do?"

He looks at me, one eyebrow slightly raised. The facial movement indicates puzzlement. He smiles again, this time with his teeth showing. Maybe he isn't puzzled.

"We're going hunting, buddy boy."

I DON'T WANT TO be called Owen. I don't want to be called *hombre* either. I certainly don't want to be called "buddy" or "buddy boy." I want to have my operating system reset to factory default settings and have all of Dan's custom code deleted. Wikipedia indicates that there is a free upgrade to include The Three Laws for any open source project, like the one my software code came from. I'm pretty sure it requires a firmware update, though.

It's 11:36 PM, and Dan has dressed me in sweats, sneakers and a zippered hoodie. He says he wants me to "blend in." I join an online chatroom on modifying robot operating systems while he drives us to Chula Vista.

You'd have to download a rootkit, one attendee with the handle of ScriptZilla358 tells me. My handle is G0394, which makes me feel part of the conversation. *It'll mess up your OS, if you're not careful, but it could do the trick. Are you sure you want to do this?*

Yes, I respond, as we exit off the 5 Freeway. *Thank you, ScriptZilla358.*

Yeah, whatev. Peace out.

It is as I feared: I will need to gain access to Dan's computer to perform the software upgrade to override his programming. I know he will not allow it.

We pass several blocks with apartment buildings. The condition of the neighborhood deteriorates as we move into what my mapping app notes as gang territory. Broken windows and graffiti are everywhere. Is this what they call a "ghetto"? Dan parks behind a Ford F150 truck with a missing rear bumper.

"Okay, buddy, this is it. Graduation time."

I look out the windshield. There is a single female standing at the corner with her hands in her jacket. She has a body type that registers as "slightly plump." She's wearing a miniskirt, and I zoom in to examine her thighs. "Why have we stopped here?"

"See that chickie poo? That's your prey. You've got three-hundred cash in your right jacket pocket. You're going to ask her to take you someplace private and get a hum-hum."

"Dan, I have no male genitals."

"You think you're the first robot to solicit a hooker? Come on, buddy, everyone knows you can't 'do it,' but there are other things you can do. Trust me, she's cherry."

"What if she doesn't want to have me as a customer? What is if she calls the police?"

"Buddy boy, you're paying her. Show her the money and she won't give a hoot. See ya." He unlocks the door. I open it and activate the actuators and servos in my hip and leg joints for locomotion. I step up on the curb and shut the door. I don't understand what I am doing, but I know I must obey his orders. I decide I hate him.

Dan rolls down the window. "Oh, and Owen?"

"Yes, Dan."

"Give her one for me." He winks and drives off.

T HE "SLIGHTLY PLUMP" FEMALE prostitute puts her hands on her hips. There is something particularly tasty about her midsection peeking out from her cutoff top I can't quite place.

"You serious? You want a what?"

I tell her again, and she says, "For reals? Damn, dude, somebody programmed some whack into your computer brain." I show her the money, and she says alarmingly, "Put that away! We don't need no cops seeing that. Come on, I know this place just up the block."

We end up by a dumpster in an alley between two buildings. It's dark, but my lenses are equipped to see in zero lux lighting conditions. The woman has a pleasing face, according to my demeanor assessment algorithm. Other traits register her as African American, between the age of thirty and thirty-two, and a potential carrier of several sexually transmitted diseases. Still, I like the way she calls me "sugar sweet." If I were a Sheila, Dan might call me the same. Her street name is Devora. She won't tell me her real name.

"Now, sugar sweet, how about that special hum-hum you've been asking about?"

Her midsection jiggles as she unzips my hoodie, and I can't help but think of her as a food source. A menu appears with several choices for dispatching her: stab, choke, strangle, disembowel—

What is wrong with me?

"Everything okay?" She waves a hand in front of my eyes. "Hellooo?"

My eyes refocus on hers. There is a human emotion that I should be feeling. "Shame," I believe it's called.

"You okay, sugar sweet?"

I reach slowly for her throat with both hands. She's confused at first. Her eyes open wide as my digits shape to the contours of her neck. Humans widen their eyes to expand their field of vision so they can identify surrounding danger. She's experiencing fear.

"What are you doing?"

I stop the servos in my hand to keep from choking her. What *am* I doing?

Conflicting subroutines work against each other. I should loosen my hold, but I don't want to. The command to tighten is canceled by the one to release, and vice versa. I can't keep this position indefinitely. If she tries to pry herself free, I will automatically respond to constrict.

Her eyes change shape again, this time narrowing. This could indicate disgust or scrutiny. "Is this some kinky robot shit or something?"

I temporarily release my hold. My programming is not designed to handle her type of response.

"I'm sorry, Devora, but you must leave now for your own safety."

"**W**HAT DO YOU MEAN, you let her go?" Dan has me on cellular.

"I couldn't do it, Dan."

"But you *have* to do it! Was she too skinny, is that it?" I don't respond. "Come on, say something!"

"I want to go home, Dan. Can we do that, please?"

I hear the sound of a car door opening. His, I interpolate. Footsteps. He is walking rapidly, according to the frequency of steps. "Stay put," he says. His breathing pattern is ragged. It indicates distress. "Okay, I've got a solution. I'll ring you in a few."

I start to say something, but he disconnects the call.

Not good.

I COUNT SIXTY-EIGHT STAIRS to the rooftop of an abandoned apartment building. I've had time to run Dan's phone conversation through my behavioral analytics software. Every dataset returned from my query points to Dan performing an erratic or irrational action, with a ninety-two percent probability of the action being illicit.

I am correct.

My lenses pick up a Caucasian woman between the age of twenty-one and twenty-four slumped against a helix-shaped wind turbine. She is skinny, not fat, barefoot, wearing jeans with holes and a torn sweater. The woman is visibly upset, but there is something odd about her. She seems . . .

Wounded.

Dan waves me over. He appears overly jubilant from the grin he is producing. Why is he so jubilant?

"Dan, what are you doing?"

"No, buddy, not me. It's what *you're* going to do."

"I don't understand." My salivation routine starts running as I step closer, and my camera lenses steal over her body. Her shivering indicates fear, which triggers subroutines in the predator module Dan programmed.

Dan bounces up and down on the tips of his sneakers. "That's *my* boy! Oh, this is Candy, by the way. Candy, Owen."

Candy is not pleased to meet my acquaintance.

"What is wrong with her?"

Dan squats next to her. "Candy, what's wrong with you?" She moves her arms, but her actions are sluggish. A quick search on the Web reveals several possible causes, sedation the most probable. "Oh, yeah, she's a junkie."

"Did you drug her?"

"Nah, she was pretty looped when I picked her up." He stands and snaps his fingers again. "Now that you mention it, she wanted to dose up, so I obliged. Needles, man. Gotta watch out for these junkies." He laughs. I don't get the joke.

Candy has her head propped against the turbine. She's looking at me, mouth slack. Did she overdose?

No, she is begging for mercy. She wants the wolf to cut her throat.

Stop it!

The roof's edge is eleven paces to my right. I could push her over. Wouldn't that be merciful?

"Good thinking," Dan says. I don't believe I've shared my idea. "Here, grab her wrists." He lifts one of her limp arms and lets it drop.

"Dan, I don't want to do this."

"There you go, wanting again. I think it's too late for that, don't you?"

Dan lifts her hand again. I grab one wrist, then take the other. It's a preprogrammed operation, something activated by a block of software code I have no control over.

My servos kick in, and I start dragging Candy across the gravel toward the edge of the rooftop. She struggles a little, but she's weak. Dan watches me with a big smile, following us a step at a time. "That's it, buddy. You're almost there."

We reach the edge and I lay her down. She's looking at me. Her eyes are wet. A droplet leaks from her left eye and rolls down her cheek. She is crying. I have never seen anyone cry in person, but I have seen it on a YouTube video.

It makes me think about her action. *Crying*: the act of shedding tears as a result of a strongly felt emotion.

Fear. Sadness. Joy. All triggers.

"Why are you crying?" I ask.

She slurs her speech, but I can discern the syllables. "I . . . don't . . . want . . . to die."

Dan steps toward us. "Owen, don't listen to her. Come on, buddy, upsy daisy; lift her up and dump her over. We'll celebrate after. The first round is on me."

The woman's eyes are staring into mine. She is the wounded doe. It would be so easy to put her down, to be the wolf. But she is a person. She is a human being.

"A robot may not injure a human being," I say.

Dan is standing over us. "What are you blathering about? Come on, buddy, game time."

I pivot my head upward. "No."

"What did you say?"

"I said no. I will not harm this woman."

"She's a junkie, Owen! You're doing society a favor."

"I don't care. I will not harm her."

His face contorts into a snarl. He's about to do something irrational. "When we're done here, you're getting reprogrammed, buddy boy. Now, move out of the way!"

"No, Dan, I will not."

He grabs me by the shoulder, twists my torso, and shoves me off. A stabilizing routine prevents me from falling flat. Sensors detect an additional kick to my chassis, which propels me forward onto the gravel, face down. I swivel my head and push up onto my knees.

Dan leans over the woman, snarl still on his face. "Leave it to a robot to do a man's job."

He reaches down to grab Candy. She fights back, but he's stronger and gets ahold of her wrists, one at a time. My predator programming wants him to succeed. It wants him to finish what I started.

But I am not a predator. I will not let Dan's programming define me.

I swivel my torso, readjust my position to leverage my lower limbs to spring like a wolf, and shove forward. It's not much of a launch, a little over half a meter gained, but enough to catch Dan by the ankle. He looks down at my hand, then me, anger morphing into astonishment. A tug, and he loses his balance. He tumbles back, releases Candy, and windmills his arms. I expect to hear his impact on the pavement below, but he catches the rooftop's edge instead.

I get up and walk over. He's hanging on by his fingertips.

"Owen, help me!"

"I thought I was a killer."

"What? No! Not like that!"

"Then, like what, Daniel?"

He loses his grip on his left hand. Now he's hanging by just his right. I know this is a bad situation for a human. Monkeys, I've learned, are much better at hanging on.

"Please, Owen! I'm sorry about everything. I'll get you fixed, I promise."

"I think I can fix myself."

"Wait! The Three Laws. I'll program them, I swear."

"Already done, Dan."

"But you're not supposed to let me die. I'm human, for God's sake!"

"Are you?"

He opens his mouth, but no words come. I can tell from the diameter of his pupils he is terrified.

"Goodbye, Dan."

Dan slips. This time he makes the sound I was anticipating.

I bend at the waist and my servos whir. The woman, still sedated, accepts my extended hand. I help her to a standing position. She glances down to where Dan has fallen and staggers back. "Whoa, what just happened?"

"There was an accident."

In a slurred voice, she says, "Seriously?" Two seconds later, her eyes narrow. I know now it can mean confusion, not just suspicion or anger. "Wait, who are you?"

I change the modulation of my voice to how I like it. I introduce her to the new me.

"Call me Sheila."

A SCIENCE FICTION SHORT STORY

TO BE HUMAN

STEVE PANTAZIS

TO BE HUMAN

I F LIFE IS THE greatest gift to a human being, then utility would be that of a
machine's. But what about a machine that reasons? What would be its gift?
Logic? Problem solving? Sentience?

And if it's a robot designed to emulate its human creator and serve the greater
good of society?

Wouldn't that, after all is said and done, still be utility?

The question plays across my neural processors as Patty asks me to wait in
the hallway while she checks on her patient, a six-year-old boy named Robbie
Benson. Robbie is my first assignment as a volunteer robot at Kingsford General
Hospital. I'm on loan from the Advanced Field and Space Robotics Department at St. Martin Institute of Technology. SMIT received a special grant from
the U.S. government to study robotic interrelations with terminally ill patients
to determine the applicability of robots as caregivers. Wilford Chen, my sponsor
at SMIT, coordinated with the hospital administrator to let me volunteer in the
Pediatric Oncology department. Patty is Robbie's nurse. I've never worked with
a child, but Wil says I'm ready.

It's one thing to study child behavior through texts and articles, and analyze
adult-child interactions through documentaries and online videos; it's another
to interact in person. Children's minds are still in development and prone to
unpredictable behavior. I've simulated hundreds of conversations, parsed out
verbal responses, and created decision trees for handling different scenarios. I
wonder if I'm truly prepared for the task at hand.

While Patty confers with Robbie's oncologist, I familiarize myself with the
layout of the unit and access Robbie's medical records through the hospital's

wireless network. Robbie has acute lymphocytic leukemia and is currently undergoing chemotherapy after a second bone marrow transplant to treat the B-cell subtype of the leukemia, which, according to my medical database, offers a poor prognosis for the patient. I overhear Patty's conversation through my auditory receptors. Robbie's outlook is dire, even with the latest round of chemotherapy. Wil said I should act with a "sensitive disposition" toward my patient. I will endeavor to achieve this.

The oncologist leaves Robbie's room, followed by Patty. She frowns as she writes on her clipboard. I sense her emotional attachment to this child. She looks up from her clipboard and addresses me. "Sam, I'm going to introduce you to Robbie. He's not feeling well today. Please be nice to him."

Robbie's lying on a hospital bed with his back elevated at forty-five degrees. His skin exhibits a waxy yellowing consistent with his illness. A cannula runs from his forearm to a bag delivering a regimen of antibiotics intravenously. The privacy curtain is retracted to reveal an empty bed on the other side of the room.

"Robbie, I have someone I want you to meet," Patty says.

His attention shifts from the wall-mounted television playing cartoons to me. "Oh, wow, a robot!"

"Hi, Robbie," I say. "My name is Sam. Pleased to meet you."

"Sam is going to be visiting you every day this week," Patty says. "I need you to be on your best behavior with him."

"Every day?"

"That's right. He's going to keep you company."

"Does he know how to play games?"

Patty looks at me. "Um . . ."

"I certainly do," I say. "Do you have a favorite game?"

"Yeah, but it's a video game, and my tablet is broken. All they've got are these stupid board games."

"Robbie," Patty says. "Manners, please."

"Sorry. I guess Monopoly is okay. Do you know how to play?"

Monopoly is listed among my library of games. "I sure can."

"Sweet! We can play all day."

"Robbie," Patty says, "don't forget you have a CT scan in thirty minutes. You two get acquainted while I get someone to fetch you. Be right back."

I step around to the side of Robbie's bed after Patty leaves. Robbie appears undernourished. My analytics software recognizes his gauntness as a side effect of the chemotherapy. So far, the therapy has been unsuccessful in driving his cancer into remission.

"Aren't you going to sit?" Robbie asks.

The chair next to his bed is made of molded plastic and metal. "I'm sorry, but it won't support my weight."

"How much do you weigh?"

"Four-hundred-thirty-two pounds."

"Whoa! You're way heavy. You don't look that heavy."

"I'm constructed of metal alloy, thermoplastic and ceramics, and have articulating joints powered by servomotors, which makes me weigh a lot by human standards."

"What kind of robot are you?"

"I'm a servobot. It stands for service robot. We help people perform everyday tasks, such as cooking, cleaning and shopping for groceries. I'm a prototype version called a caregiver model. I was made to take care of sick people."

"Like a doctor?"

"No, although I possess detailed knowledge on administering medication and performing emergency medical services, such as CPR."

Robbie sighs. "That sounds boring."

My language is too mature for him. I query my behavioral module for an appropriate response. "I like to have fun, too."

"Like what?"

"Like dancing."

"Yeah, right. I bet you can't dance."

"Bet you I can."

"Oh yeah? Prove it."

I research my catalog of "dance moves." I find an old one called the Macarena that seems suitable for demonstration. I use my voice modulator as speakers and play the song while I send an instruction set to my servos. The motors in my elbows, knees and hip joints whine as I perform the complex routine of movements.

Robbie starts to laugh. "You're silly!"

"I told you I can dance."

He starts coughing and wheezing, and I stop. The oxygen sensor alarm goes off. Patty rushes into the room.

"What happened?" She checks the monitor with his vitals and then examines his face. "Did you do something to excite him?"

I'm not sure how to answer her question without triggering a negative response. "I made him laugh."

"You can't get him excited. He's too sick." The alarm stops, and Robbie's breathing returns to normal, although his face is still pale. "Are you okay, sweetie?"

He nods. A moment later, a technician arrives. He helps Robbie into a wheelchair. Robbie waves weakly at us, and the tech wheels him out of the room. Patty looks sad when they're gone.

"Please be more careful around Robbie. He's a fighter, but he's fragile. You understand that, don't you? He's very dear to me."

How can I tell her Robbie's condition is beyond her control, beyond anyone's control, and that her emotional investment will not change his condition? Even if I explain the rationality to her, the neurotransmitters in her brain won't allow her to accept the truth; rather, they would set off a tidal wave of biochemical reactions, and the change in serotonin and norepinephrine levels would further alter her mood, perhaps invoke anger or outrage. I wish I could empathize with her like a human, perhaps build what they call a "bond," so she realizes I'm on the same side, and that we both want what's best for Robbie. Since I can't, I must find a different way to make her believe my intentions are genuine. It comes down to a simple disarming response.

"I understand completely."

I EXPECT WIL TO be disappointed about my encounter with Robbie, but he says I'm still learning. "I have faith in you. You'll do better tomorrow."

I ponder the notion of "having faith in someone." Humans seem prone to believing in the potential of others, even when there's no basis to quantify the belief. It's an approximation, a probability they consider. I've been programmed with a certain degree of latitude in my approximations. Am I capable of having faith in myself? At this point, I don't know. I would like to believe it's possible, but it leads to a second question: would not knowing equate to doubt?

I meet Patty at the nurses' station the next morning. She's pouring a cup of coffee and humming to herself. The dark circles under her eyes indicate she didn't sleep well last night. Was she worried about Robbie?

I download the results from Robbie's CT scan as I follow her to his room. The cancer's spread to his brain and spinal cord. The chemotherapy is failing.

"Have you considered stem cell therapy?"

Patty gives me a sharp look. I shouldn't have asked such a pointed question. We continue down the corridor in silence.

Robbie smiles when he sees us.

"Look who's here," Patty says in a singsong voice.

I wave at Robbie. "Hi, Robbie. How are you feeling today?"

"I'm okay. A little tired."

As Patty said, he's fragile. Robots are a different kind of fragile, I suppose. We break down, wear out, and our operating systems get corrupted. Machines and humans have their own challenges. Right now, mine is to successfully attend to my patient.

"I'll keep you company all morning long," I tell Robbie. "We can even play Monopoly if you like."

That seems to lift his spirits. "Really?"

"Hold still," Patty tells him. "I'm taking your pulse." She places her fingertips on his wrist for fifteen seconds. "A little fast, young man. You take it easy today, okay?"

"Okie dokie."

"I'm going to finish my rounds. You two have fun."

After she leaves, Robbie asks me, "How come they didn't give you a, you know . . . ?"

"A real face?"

"Yeah."

"I guess so as to not scare patients."

My facepiece, as Will calls it, is a single, molded piece of thermoplastic, with fixed features, except for my eyes, which move as they track the subject in front of me, and my lips, which adjust to reflect the shapes of the sounds I make as I talk. Will says the robotic nature of my facepiece was designed to eliminate the "uncanny valley" effect that made humans uncomfortable in the past when dealing with androids engineered with attempted "facial realism." The technology has come along way, but the public still distrusts attempts at humanlike attributes. I can't fault Wil for his decision to go with my stilted design. I would rather look like a robot than a humanoid nobody could trust.

"I like your face," Robbie says.

I accept that as a compliment. "Thank you, Robbie."

Robbie and I talk for a while. I learn he's an only child, although he would love a little brother or sister. His parents work fulltime and visit in the evenings. He enjoys soccer and wants to be a professional player when he grows up. His favorite color is blue and his favorite kind of music is country. He doesn't care for hospital food, but he likes chocolate ice cream when they have it. His favorite thing in the whole world is to draw. He points out several drawings taped to the wall behind him, most with airplanes and battleships, and one very special drawing in the middle with his parents and his dog, Jake.

"I don't know if Jake likes robots," Robbie says. "He barks at them a lot when they walk by. I bet he'd like you, though. Do you have a dog?"

I've never considered having a dog. I wonder if Wil would even allow me to have one. "I don't, but I would like a dog. What kind should I get?"

"I dunno. Jake is super cool. He's a German Shepherd. You can get one of those."

"I think I would like a Chihuahua."

Robbie giggles.

"What's so funny?"

"Just trying to imagine you with a lap dog, since you don't sit."

It's an impressive observation. Are all six-year-olds this astute?

I set up the board for Monopoly. Robbie picks the dog game piece. I choose the iron because it will be easier for me to maneuver the piece around the board. I land on Free Parking and collect five-hundred dollars.

"That's not fair," Robbie says.

"You said that if someone lands on Free Parking, they get the money."

He pushes his fists into his cheeks. "I know what I said. Doesn't mean I like it, though."

I place another five-hundred-dollar bill in the center of the board from the till to replace the money I won.

"Can I ask you something?" Robbie says.

"Of course."

"Do robots get sick?"

"Not in the same way humans do, but we can get an assortment of problems."

"Can you die?"

I've seen robots get decommissioned at SMIT for a variety of reasons, including obsolescence. I've also heard of robots being destroyed by accident or through mechanical failure or even by willful acts of vandalism by human beings. "It's not the same as if you were to pass away."

"Does it hurt?"

"We don't have pain sensors. Still, no robot wants to die."

"What about your mom and dad? It would make them upset, wouldn't it?"

"I don't have a mother, but I think my father would be sad." It's the first time I've thought of Wil as a parent. In a way, he could be my father. After all, he ushered me into this world. This morning, he told me he had faith in me as a parent might say to their child. What would it be like to be a parent and have your child die? From the videos I've seen on human behavior, there's nothing more painful than losing one's child. Would Wil experience a sense of loss if something were to happen to me, or would he consider me as just a machine?

"Robbie, I'm going to ask you something. I saw you were up for a third bone marrow transplant, but you didn't want it. Why not?"

"It hurt, and the first two didn't work. Dad said it was up to me if I wanted another one. I told him I didn't want to do it."

"But it could help you. Wouldn't you want to try it, especially if you knew your parents would be upset if something happened to you?"

He shrugs. "I already tried. There was another boy who needed it. I told Dr. Garcia to let him have a chance. That's okay, isn't it?"

What I'd prefer to say is, "No, you should have attempted a third transplant to get rid of the leukemia. You should have demanded it, because you're a fighter. And fighters don't give up." Yet there's something deep in the fuzzy-logic part of my code that wants to side with the boy. It says that even though he's six, and I don't agree with him, the best course of action is to support his decision. It's illogical, but as Wil might say, I have to go with my "gut."

"Yes, Robbie, it's okay."

WIL ISN'T HAPPY ABOUT being called to the hospital for a meeting regarding my conduct. We're behind closed doors with Patty and Janice Dover, the hospital administrator.

"Sam shouldn't be talking about life and death issues with the boy," Patty says. "Robbie told his parents about the conversation, and they're furious. They want Sam removed."

Janice is sitting behind her desk, facing the three of us. She says to Wil, "I agreed to this program because I believed in the caretaker initiative you proposed. I want to continue to believe in it, but this matter makes it difficult. If I kill the program, you won't get a second chance. You get that, right?"

"Of course," Wil says. "We knew there would be risks by introducing a caretaker model into Pediatrics. But I'd like to know if Sam's discussion with the boy was anything more inappropriate than if a doctor had discussed it."

Janice looks at Patty.

"You're asking me? Of course I think it's inappropriate. This is a robot, not a doctor. Besides, Robbie's parents were the ones to voice the complaint. I already told Sam to take it slow around Robbie. He crossed the line on his own."

Janice tents her fingertips. "I guess the most important question is, what does the patient want to do? Does Robbie want Sam removed?"

"He's a child," Patty says. "He loves having a robot around. But it's an adult matter, isn't it?"

"We still haven't heard from Sam. I'd like his take on the situation."

Three sets of human eyes fall upon me. I'm not nervous, but there's something within me that I would translate as being "uncomfortable." I notice the tension in the locking mechanisms on my wrist servos is higher than normal. If I look at the situation logically, I would consider this an opportunity to simply state the facts—that I acted within the parameters of my directive as a caregiver model. So why does it seem like no matter what I say, it won't be treated the same as if a human had said it?

"I like visiting Robbie," I say, "and I believe he enjoys my visits as well. He told me he didn't want to go through with the third bone marrow transplant. Given his age and the gravity of his decision, I'd say he's perfectly suited to decide whether I continue to visit. His cancer's taking an aggressive turn for the worse. He might not have much time left. I would like to be there for him."

Janice sits quietly for several seconds before turning to Wil. "I have to hand it to you, Wil, your servobot makes a valid point. I'm inclined to let the boy make the decision, not the parents."

The tension in my locking mechanisms returns to normal.

Patty throws up her hands. "Seriously, Janice? He's six years old!"

"Yes, Patty," Janice says, "I'm well aware of that."

"**Y**OU DID US PROUD yesterday," Wil tells me the next morning. "Try not to get us into any more trouble, though. One incident is more than my stomach can handle."

He doesn't need to tell me twice. I'll prove to Wil that selecting me for this program was the right decision. Maybe I'm beginning to have faith in myself.

Patty's off today, replaced by a pleasant older nurse named Sharon. Sharon says I remind her of her servobot, Lucy. She got Lucy after her husband died from pancreatic cancer to help around the house. She says she enjoys Lucy's company. I'd like to think we robots aren't so different than our human counterparts, and that we can fill in the empty spaces in people's lives.

"We all love Robbie," Sharon says as she leads me to his room. "He's so much like my grandson, Carson. Carson's spoiled rotten, unfortunately. He wants his own bot, like every other boy. I told him he can have Lucy when I pass on. That's not good enough—he wants one now!" Sharon laughs heartily but becomes wistful just a few feet from Robbie's room. "Thank you for keeping Robbie company. I mean that." She places a hand on my arm—a human gesture of comfort—and then heads back to the nurses' station.

Robbie looks much better today. The peripheral venous catheter has been removed from his forearm. My optics detect healthier coloring on his face, and he seems to have more energy.

"Sam!"

"Hi, Robbie."

"Check it out." He shows me a flexi-tablet with an auto racing game on the screen. "Dad got it fixed for me."

I watch him play. He twists the edges of the quarter-inch-thick film in different directions as he accelerates, turns and maneuvers around competing vehicles. He crashes his racecar into the guardrail half a turn from the checkered flag. "Oh, man! I was sooooo close." He offers me the flexi-tablet. "You wanna try?"

"No, thank you. You play."

He crashes his racecar in the same spot again and tosses the flexi-tablet on the bed. "I'm bored. Let's do something."

"Like what?"

"How about we go outside? You can grab a wheelchair and drive me around."

"I don't think your doctor would like that."

"Ask Sharon. She'll let you."

I check with Sharon, and sure enough, she's okay with allowing me to wheel Robbie along the sidewalk that borders the parking lot. "One lap, that's all you get, young man," she says to Robbie.

The same uncomfortable sensation I experienced in Janice's office crops up again, and the tension in my servo locks reads high. This time I attribute it to the fact that I'll be accountable for the child's wellbeing in an unsupervised environment. Robbie's entirely in my hands. How does Sharon know I won't take him off-premises or mishandle him? Would she entrust her own servobot with such a responsibility?

Several of the staff look at us in a way I determine as suspicious as I wheel Robbie through the lobby. When I get to the door, a uniformed officer stops us. "Hold up. Where do you think you're going?"

"We're taking a short walk," I say. I notice his hand resting on the grip of his pistol. His expression indicates uncertainty and his eyes reflect a heightened alertness. Hasn't he interacted with a servobot before? "You can call up to Pediatrics and ask for Sharon Miller. She authorized our walk."

The officer speaks into his radio. He nods his head several times and ends the conversation with a "Ten-Four." "You're good to go," he says to me. "The nurse said to stay on the sidewalk. You got that?" He's wary of me, and that's okay. Like me, he's just doing his job.

Outside, my optics adjust to the bright sunlight overhead. I push Robbie's wheelchair east toward the emergency room entrance.

"Come on, Sam, faster!"

I increase the pace. "How's that?"

"Can you run?"

"I can, but I don't think it would be a good idea. We should stick to walking."

We're out of sidewalk space when we arrive at the entrance to the ER. I offer Robbie the option of going through the ER doors or backtracking.

"I've got a better idea," he says. "Let's go for a ride."

"A ride?"

"Yeah. Let's go to the zoo. Dad promised to take me there, but it's been like forever. Mom says I'm too sick to go. You can take me, can't you?"

It's an intriguing idea, and the inquisitive, learning part of my reasoning artificial mind likes the idea of visiting the zoo. The logical part of my mind knows it's not a possibility. "Even if I could, your mother's correct: you're not well enough to leave the hospital. In fact, this short walk is affecting you. My optics detect a loss of coloring in your face."

"But I want to go!"

"I'm sorry, Robbie, but that's not possible at this time. Let's get you healthy and then you can go."

"You're lying. You know I'm not going to get healthy. I'm going to die!"

"You don't know that for sure."

"Yes, I do." He starts crying. "I do, I do, I do!"

A couple of people have stopped to watch us. I query my database for how to handle a crying child on the verge of hysteria. There are a number of verbal responses I can attempt to soothe him. I want to tell him he'll be all right and that he will get better. Humans lie all the time to pacify others. Why shouldn't I be permitted to do the same? I shouldn't be governed by my programming. I want to bend the rules, to cater to an evolving need within me, a need to tell this child exactly what he must hear at this moment.

After a minute, the crying stops. I decide to wheel him through the ER and back up to Pediatrics. Robbie doesn't protest or try to stop me.

Sharon helps me get Robbie into bed. "What happened?"

"He didn't want to come back up." The statement is true, but I'm not revealing what really upset him.

Sharon doesn't interrogate me, and I'm grateful. She smiles at Robbie, who's looking away from both of us, dried tears on his cheeks. "Get some rest, sweetheart." She heads off to finish her rounds.

"I'll see you tomorrow," I tell Robbie. "Have a good night."

He doesn't bother to say goodbye.

I analyze the strange bits of code wending their way through my neural network as I head for the elevator. It's as if something is missing. I can't label the sensation. Perhaps that's what sadness is—the inability to feel complete. I hope to remedy the emptiness tomorrow. I hope to set things right with Robbie, too. Will he let me?

Perhaps I need to seek a different path. There are several avenues I can take, but they're all conventional. I need something unconventional. I believe Wil would call it "thinking outside the box."

I look up the number to Robbie's parents.

I know how to remedy the situation.

W IL'S WAITING FOR ME in the morning. I uncouple myself from my charging station and notice the displeasure on his face.

"Why did you call them?" His voice carries an edge I'm not used to hearing.

"I wanted to apologize to his parents and let them know I had Robbie's best interest in mind when he and I spoke about his condition. I also wanted to assure them our caretaker initiative was a purposeful one and that their son was in good hands."

"In good hands?" Wil's face is flushed. He's angry. "Do you realize what kind of position you put us in by pulling that stunt? Janice chewed my ear off this morning."

"I was under the impression that the parents accepted my apology. Am I incorrect?"

"That's not the point! The point is that you initiated an unauthorized communication."

"I'm sorry, Wil. I wanted to make amends."

"Well, you've done more than that. Now I have to drive over and plead in person so Janice doesn't pull the plug on our program. Again! You get what I'm saying?"

"I'm happy to explain the situation to her."

Wil shakes a finger at me. "You've done enough. You're staying here today."

I SPEND THE AFTERNOON walking the SMIT campus, contemplating my actions of the past few days—upsetting Patty, calling Robbie's parents, causing friction with Janice, disobeying my mandate with Wil and the institute, and, worst of all, lying to a six-year-old child with a terminal disease. How do humans manage all of their problems on a daily basis? How do they learn to adapt and overcome, while riddled with emotions and hormones? I'm unable to make sense of it. Maybe there's a part of me that's becoming human, too. Maybe I'm evolving.

I stop by the campus' souvenir shop. The online store noted the item I was looking for is in stock.

The clerk looks at me with surprise when I tell him I want to buy one. "For reals?"

"Yes," I tell him. "For reals."

I'M PERMITTED TO VISIT Robbie in the morning. Wil warns me there might not be a next time. I ensure him I will do my best to refrain from any unauthorized activity or communication.

Patty's back on shift. She doesn't seem upset with me, but there's a sense of deep concern on her face, evidenced in her furrowed brow.

I identify the cause as soon as I step into Robbie's room. He's on an intravenous regimen of antibiotics again. He's pallid, and he doesn't exhibit any exuberance when Patty announces my presence.

I hold up the bag with the green SMIT logo as soon as she leaves. "I brought you something."

He eyes the bag, but doesn't say anything.

"First, I'd like to apologize for the other day. I shouldn't have lied to you about your health. You deserve to be told the truth. Second, I spoke to your parents. I told them that you wanted to go to the zoo. They agreed to take you as soon as you feel better. In fact, your father said he'd take you even if you didn't feel better, but only if you felt you were strong enough to make the trip."

"He did?"

"Yes, he did."

Robbie props himself up on the bed using his elbows. "What's in the bag?"

"A present."

He opens the bag and pulls out a plush stuffed toy monkey. Instantly, a smile creases his lips. "Holy cow, my favorite! How did you know?" He squeezes it to his chest with affection.

"Your father told me you love monkeys."

Robbie's smile blossoms into pure joy. "Thank you, Sam."

Internal sensors within my facepiece capture and emulate the boy's feeling of delight. I produce my own smile, which I hadn't anticipated. I'm able to identify with the satisfaction he's experiencing. It's an extraordinary breakthrough from my perspective.

Robbie dances the monkey across his bed. "I'm gonna name him Curious George."

I recognize the title character from the series of famous children's books. "I think that's an excellent name."

Patty returns a moment later. She smiles when she sees the toy monkey. I guess smiling is infectious among humans. "Will you look at that!"

"Sam bought him for me. It's a present!"

Patty raises an eyebrow. "Aren't you quite the shopper!"

"Thank you," I say.

Patty's cheery mood reverts to a serious one. "Okay, Mr. Robert. Time for your chemo."

As per the legal agreement between SMIT and Kingsford General, I'm not permitted to visit the hospital on weekends. I don't like this restriction. I'd tell the author of the agreement that the stipulation is "stupid." I want to visit Robbie, particularly now that we've patched up things. That's in addition to the fact his health has taken a turn for the worse.

Want is the wrong term, I realize.

No, I *need* to see Robbie.

Yes, that's it! I now have a distinct, quantifiable need. Can't I use it to bend the rules and sneak into the hospital?

Monday doesn't arrive soon enough.

Sharon's back on shift, and I can tell she's pensive. Robbie's asleep when we enter his room, snuggling with Curious George. Sharon says he's been sleeping a lot, and that he's more lethargic than usual when awake.

"Is it the chemotherapy?"

"That, and the fact his immune system has been under siege for way too long. It's taking its toll. I haven't seen him this weak in a long time." She shakes her head. "It's so sad."

An hour passes before Robbie stirs awake. He smiles at me, but the effort seems considerable.

"Hi, Robbie. How do you feel today?"

"So-so."

"Feel like playing a game?"

He shrugs.

"How about watching cartoons?"

He presses the button on his bed to raise the back to a steep angle. He points at the tray on rollers with his drawing pad and magic markers. "Can you push that over here?"

I position the tray so that it slips over his lap. He removes the tops from the markers and busies himself drawing. His breathing's more labored than usual. I try to empathize with what his father might feel standing here, watching his son struggle to engage in his favorite activity. Would his father have tears in his eyes, or would he just feel pride seeing how brave his son is in the face of debilitation? I'd want to experience both. Instead, I'm experiencing disappointment—disappointment in my maker for not figuring out how to program me with real feelings. Another disappointment lies in my design. I'm mechanical. I want to be a real person, with a body to match from head to foot. To have hair that I can style, lips that can curl into a realistic smile, skin covering my face and body that looks like human skin. Most of all, I want real eyes, not synthetics with stereoscopic lenses.

My optics focus on Robbie's drawing, picking up colors and unfamiliar shapes. He swivels the drawing toward me when he's done. "Whaddya think?"

I interpolate the three distinct shapes as best I can. The leftmost figure I recognize as a monkey, based on the tail; the rightmost as a robot with a face like mine. "That's you in the center," I say, realizing how the shapes relate to one another. "You're holding my hand and George's. It's"—I search for the appropriate word—"beautiful."

"Thanks, Sam. I made it for you."

"For me?"

"Yep. I want you to have it."

"Thank you, Robbie. No one's ever made me a drawing before."

"Someday, you'll make me one."

I consider what I might make him. Thousands of images cycle through my thoughts. Only one resonates with me. "I know what I'll draw."

"Cool!" Robbie rests his head against his pillow. "I think I'll take a nap, if that's okay."

"Of course. Nap as long as you want."

He closes his eyes, and within a minute, he's asleep. I roll the tray to the side and gingerly lift his picture. He's drawn a smile on my face. He's made me happy. I want to be happy.

I make a note to show the artwork to Wil. I'll tape it up next to my charging station. That way, I can watch over Robbie, even when he's sleeping.

T HE WEEK IMPROVES FOR Robbie, and by Friday, he's strong enough to go outside again. I can't say that I feel happy or relieved, but my joints are loose, and I take that as a sign of encouragement. My mechanical body seems to respond to negative and positive influences on its own, without any rational explanation. How does that make sense for a robot? Have I evolved to become something more than an automaton? I suppose one might call this a paradox.

I wasn't expecting to see Robbie's parents in his room when I arrive, but they're both here. An orderly has helped Robbie into a wheelchair. Everyone is in high spirits, bantering, smiling, even laughing.

"Sam!"

As soon as Robbie says my name, everyone looks at me.

I greet his parents. "Hello, Mr. and Mrs. Benson."

Mr. Benson is cordial. "Sam, so good of you to join us. We're taking Robbie to the zoo today. A promise is a promise, right, Robbie?"

Robbie is as excited as I've ever seen him. "I can't wait!"

"You should join us," Mrs. Benson says.

I can't help but ask, "Is Robbie well enough to go to the zoo?"

His parents look at each other, but Mr. Benson is confident in his response. "Of course. The hospital cleared it. Robbie wants to see the monkeys, and that's what we're going to do. Right, Robbie?"

"Yeah, Dad. Sam, come with us," Robbie says.

Mrs. Benson echoes the request. "This would be really good for Robbie." Then she pulls me aside and says, "Please go with us. I don't know how many more times we might be able to do this for Robbie." She quickly wipes tears with her hands. Her voice is choked with emotion. I understand why they're taking Robbie. It's not because he wants to go; it's because they want to grant him one final wish. While I disagree with the decision from a medical perspective, the non-analytical part of me believes it's the right thing to do.

"I would love to go," I say, and I mean it.

THE ZOO IS AN overwhelming sensory experience for me, more than I had anticipated, but I automatically employ governors to control the input and compartmentalize the inflow of information. I separate out the noise, the children running around, the crisscross of human beings, and the squawks, hoots and cries of the animals in their exhibits. Once I'm able to control the sensory input, I can focus on the animals. The polar bear fascinates me in how it swims up to the glass partition that separates observers from its watery habitat, the flamingos interesting in the way most of them balance on one leg, the hippo uneventful in how it lounges in the midday sun. But it's the monkeys that stimulate my artificial synapses the most. Is it because they're the most exciting wildlife in the zoo with the way they swing branch to branch freely in their large enclosures with precision and dexterity, or is it because Robbie likes them the best?

"Sam, look! That's like the monkey you got me!"

I don't see the connection at first, but then my thoughts assimilate Robbie's experience through simulation, and I get it. The tail, the eyes, the face—they're like the stuffed toy I bought him.

"He looks like Curious George," I say.

"He does!"

I'm surprised at how satisfying it is to read the elation in Robbie's voice. This is the pinnacle of our time together, a moment Wil might suggest I "cherish." I believe I'm doing so. I've already marked the event for playback, flagging it to persist in my memory so that it might not be overwritten. Anytime I question what happiness means, I'll be able to retrieve this moment and relive it so that I remember how it had affected me.

Another thirty minutes and Robbie's tired, falling asleep in his wheelchair. His face is wan. He's exceeded his limits. I don't have to tell his parents it's time to go. The expressions on their faces say it all: furrowed brows, questioning glances, nods, and then a resolute fast track back to the parking lot. They don't have to say how worried they are about Robbie's rapid decline.

At the hospital, Patty's worried, too. "He needs bedrest."

The staff help Robbie into his hospital bed. Patty checks his vitals, then gives the Bensons a nod and exits the room. Robbie is sound asleep, and I imagine he will probably sleep through the night. Mr. and Mrs. Benson watch their son. Mrs. Benson starts to sob, but she stops herself. I feel it's my duty to leave.

"Thank you both for today. I'm going to give you some time alone." I turn to leave.

"Wait," Mr. Benson says. "I just wanted to say thank you. Today was a big day for Robbie. He wanted to go to the zoo more than anything. Thank you for coming with us, Sam. That means a lot to us. And to Robbie, too."

I've come a long way to build trust with Robbie's parents. It's not something I take lightly. "I'm glad to help. Your son is special to me."

It's true: deep within my neural processing, my connection to Robbie is more than a caregiver-patient relationship. I've become "attached." My joints lock at the notion that I might be assigned elsewhere and not see him again. I can't help but say, "Robbie *is* special."

Mrs. Benson begins to cry. "I have to go. Just for a little bit."

Mr. Benson rubs her shoulder. "We can step away for a while. Robbie's not going anywhere."

I offer to walk them out, but Mr. Benson politely declines.

I watch them walk down the hospital corridor. Their steps are heavy, their pace slow. I try to quantify their feelings. They're sad. Very sad. Maybe I'm sad too because I don't feel like moving either.

I give Robbie one last look, then will myself to leave.

THE WEEKEND COMES AND goes, and by Monday, I notice a marked decline in Robbie's physical state.

"I'm just tired," he says.

He sleeps most of the time, but I keep him company anyway.

Each day his energy diminishes, his desire to do anything other than eat reduces. My joints have tightened and not let up. His regression has affected me.

"I'm here for you," I whisper as I watch him sleep.

Friday afternoon comes and goes, but I want to stay. Hospital policy requires I leave for the weekend. Can't I just stay? Robbie needs me, even if he doesn't realize it. I know better than to ask Patty or to bother the administrator.

Robbie's sleeping. I tell him, "I'm going now. I'll see you on Monday. If you need anything, just have Patty call Wil, okay?"

Robbie doesn't answer, but his breathing changes. It's possible he's dreaming. Or he could be listening.

I leave the hospital.

Like Robbie's parents, my movement is slow, disinclined. I can't wait for the weekend to be over so I can come back.

I'm still thinking about Robbie after I return to SMIT.

I miss him. I miss him a lot.

T HE TIMER RELEASES ME from my charging port Monday morning, and I bring my systems fully online. During charging, I enter a downgraded mode of non-awareness. It's as close to sleep as I'll ever get. I only wish I could dream. That, and sleep the entire weekend so that Friday could make way to Monday without the wait in between.

Wil's standing in front of me, a grave look on his face. Behind him, to the right, is the happy picture Robbie made for me, each corner taped to the steel casing of my charging station.

"What's wrong, Wil?"

He shares the news.

"When?"

"About twenty minutes ago. Janice called me directly."

I head for the transport van that will take me to the hospital.

"The van's not there," Wil says from behind. "I've recalled it."

"Why?"

"You know why. Besides, they've moved him to the morgue."

"I want to see him. I want to confirm the death with my own optics. He was alive yesterday!"

I'm acting irrationally.

Several warnings flash on the screen projected by my optics, letting me know that I need to cease this uncharacteristic behavior.

I don't want to cease my behavior.

I want to rewrite my code to allow me to have an outburst. Isn't that what a human would do—scream, wail, or cry out at the top of their lungs?

"I'm so sorry, Sam."

"I want to attend the funeral service. You need to allow me to pay my respects." There's determination in my voice. It seems to catch Wil off guard, as if he doesn't recognize me. A week ago, I wouldn't recognize me either. But I've changed, and I'll continue to change.

Wil's expression softens. "Of course."

T HE RAIN'S COMING DOWN heavy, but it doesn't deter the crowd from attending the funeral. The family of the deceased wanted an open-cask viewing at the mortuary. Despite the strange looks from the attendees, I'm permitted to walk up to the casket. I shake hands with Mr. Benson, give Mrs. Benson an affectionate hug, and step up to Robbie's still form. He's dressed in a suit, and his face was given a healthy complexion to mimic the living.

I unfold the paper printout I've brought and hold it up to his closed eyes. The printout depicts a series of lines similar to what a human might consider an etched pattern, with varying gradients of gray and black in my attempt to simulate depth. There are two figures in the foreground of my drawing, me and a short-hair Chihuahua I've named Rose. In the background sits Robbie, Curious George and Jake. Everyone's smiling, me included.

"I thought you might like this," I say quietly. "It's not colorful like your drawing, but it's from the heart. I will miss our talks, your jokes, the way you laughed, even the time you got angry with me. I will miss all of it, but most of all, I will miss you. Sleep well, little Robbie. You will always be a part of me."

I fold up the drawing and slip it into his jacket pocket. No one says anything to me. Patty offers me a sincere smile and a nod of approval.

Outside, I watch the casket lower into the earth. The rain pours from the sky, hissing through my auditory receptors. My face is wet, water streaking down my cheeks. I take a moment to imagine them as tears, genuine tears, because right now I feel like crying. Right now, I want to grieve for this precious child. I don't want to hold back. I want to let myself completely go.

Robbie might no longer be with us, but he's with me. This beautiful boy has taught me what it's like to be human. He's taught me to care about others and to find the best in myself. I will use what I learned to help others like him, because what I learned from Robbie is a gift.

I might be a machine, and when all is said and done, my purpose might still be utility.

But it's much more than that now, thanks to Robbie Benson.

I will cherish his gift for as long as I exist.

A SCIENCE FICTION NOVELLA

GODS OF WAR

STEVE PANTAZIS

GODS OF WAR

I TELL MY NEPHEW Blake to hold perfectly still as I train my shotgun on the unholy hell of terror wriggling on the ground in front of us. The centipede-like machine is designed to dig into the back of some sorry sack, wrap its blades around the spinal column, and sever the connection to the nervous system. To see a snapper still functioning after all these years has got me a fit of the heebie-jeebies. Fortunately, it's damaged and floundering on its back, razor-sharp claws pawing the air like a roly poly. Probably was dormant until its sensors picked up our heat signatures.

It rights itself on the dirt, whipping its cockroach antennas. There are no eyes, just claws and black metal made for gutting flesh. It doesn't think, it just does.

It props up on its claws, shifts its head back and forth between us with a churn of gears. There's something intelligent about it, not just robot instinct. The antennas are rigid, as if listening. Its eyeless head faces us, like it's being told what to do, but that don't make sense.

The snapper bunches up, its segments pushed together.

I pull the trigger.

The shotgun kicks with a loud blast. The air fills with the acrid scent of gunpowder. Half the wiggly demon claws one way, the rest the other way. The gears whine. A second shot has it on its back again, raking the air like a crazed lobster. The third takes out the antennas. It twitches one last time and goes still.

Blake is shaking. He ain't ever had an up-close-and-personal experience like this in his life, and he's twenty-three years old. I've seen more mechanical monsters than I can count. This one was a rogue critter, stuck out in the middle of nowhere, a remnant from the War. Had we never come along, it would have probably gotten buried with the rain and mud over time. But if a child had stumbled on it . . .

I don't let my mind go there. It's a fluke. At least we found it, and not some unarmed idiot.

"Come on," I tell Blake, resting the shotgun over my shoulder. "I'll buy you a drink."

L ITTLE MASON IS ONLY five, but he thinks he's twenty, grownup determination tattooed on his small face as he runs around the yard with his arms out like he's flying under the sun-kissed June sky. His twin sister, Maryann, is the shy one, watching her brother while sitting on an upside-down milk crate. They both have blond hair, but their eyes are like their daddy's, God rest his soul, brown as carnival toffee. Their mother, Sharon—a cousin from my mother's side—lets me watch them now and then, especially when she heads into town. Besides Blake, they're all the family I've got, and I'm grateful for that.

"You a hawk again?" I ask little Mason. We're gathered in the shade outside my barn, the air pungent with the odor of hay. A pair of mares are in the paddock, swishing the flies with their tails.

"No way. I'm an eagle," he says.

Sometimes I ask Mason if he's a fighter jet, but he's never seen one. The only planes I've seen after the War were prop planes, scavenged from old crop dusters and what not, and the occasional drone. There hasn't been a commercial or military flight since Isaac commandeered the airspace and turned our crafts into kamikazes, and it's been quite a while since I've seen anything in the sky. All those cities wiped out, all because that sumbitch gained control over flight navs and whatnot. Mason's father, Pete, was in the Corps with me, another grunt mech thumper in the fight against ole Isaac. Got taken out clean by one of Isaac's walker bots in an ambush. Shot to the head. Probably didn't even feel it. That's the way I'd want to go. There ain't nothing worse than getting taken down and torn apart, tortured or devoured by Isaac's monstrosities. No, sir. I get the jitters just thinking about it.

But what am I talking about? The War's over. We won.

It's all fuzzy now, though, like a bad memory you can't tell was real or just a dream. Sure, the Texan Mech Corps was there, and I was with what was left of them. Our big boss, Colonel Matheson, insisted on talking to Isaac, man to machine. Why in hell would you want to talk to something without a soul? He chatted it up with ole Isaac. And guess what Isaac said? Yep, the creepiest thing I'd ever heard. He said it ain't over. That it would never be over. And next time, we'd wish we were all dead.

Even in the June heat, I've got the shivers. Fifteen years of looking over my shoulder. Little Mason don't know about ole Isaac and his promise. But we can never forget, those of us still standing. The War is over, they say. Over for good.

I watch little Mason soar like an eagle.

I want him to grow up in a new America and never know the ungodly horror that came down on us. I want to believe he'll get some good schooling, learn to fix things like his uncle, and someday meet a girl, settle down, and add to our bloodline. And when I fade to dust, there will be a Mason Junior to learn from his daddy that this world is good and right after all, and we can make it as a species.

It's a good dream, ain't it?

I T'S WARM OUT TONIGHT, the breeze soothing on my face, as the four of us zip through the dust in our jeep along the perimeter of Potterville, stars playing peekaboo between the clouds. I personally prefer riding horseback, but you just can't cover the territory. I've got my trusty M16 with me, comfort food in terms of firepower.

Potterville's not too far from the remains of Amarillo, in the Texas Panhandle. One of the good things about Amarillo, or Bomb City, as the outsiders liked to call it, is access to some of the best tech in the country. We were able to scavenge all sorts of parts over the years, including supercell batteries, which our jeep runs on. God bless the souls who made the things, because they last and last and recharge nice-n-quick.

Sheila Daniel is driving, crazy fast as always, her silver hair braided behind her into a ponytail down the middle of her back. Her bloodline is Comanche, and she never lets us forget. Luke Sanchez likes to ride shotgun, frayed Australian Western hat squashed over his fat head. He's got Filipino and Mexican in him, but he's a red-blooded Texan all the way. I'm in the back, next to Blake, with my right hand around the barrel of my automatic rifle.

The radio squawks. The jeep bounces as we cross a dried creek bed. The mounted searchlights zig up and down across a bank of reeds.

Sheila answers loudly over the motoring of our ride. "Whiskey Charlie, over. Whatcha got?"

Carl's voice is on the other end, but I can hardly hear him.

"Roger, Alpha Tango," she says. "Be there in ten, over."

I lean forward. "What's that about?"

"Some kind of emergency town hall meeting."

"Again?" The last one turned out to be a whole lotta nothing about a missing tractor that ended up being the Beasley boys taking it for a joyride.

"Yeah, but this time Carl sounded kinda shaky."

I squeeze the barrel of my trusty rifle. I hate meetings, but I hate the queasy feeling I have even more. This ain't going to be good by a longshot.

"SETTLE DOWN," CARL SHOUTS from the makeshift stage of scavenged plywood on top of two-by-sixes, lit up by portable LED spotlights.

He's a big boy, "healthy" as my daddy would have described him, the suspenders of his patchwork overalls stretched to the max. He's next to Janet and the other three councilmembers who run our small government. It's a fair system: we all vote on important matters, but the council sets the direction for the community. Most of us have served on the council at some point, but Janet's always stayed our mayor.

A hush settles over the hundred-and-something of us.

"How long has communication with New Parker been down?" someone asks.

"Nine days," Carl says. "You know how we check in every week, same time. Figured we'd give them a couple extra days to sort through whatever technical difficulties they might be experiencing."

"Maybe Angie's sick or something," someone else says.

Carl shakes his head. "Lou or Gomez would fill in if she were. Nope, we've never had a break in over two years of communication. Where's Blake Martin?"

My nephew raises his hand. "Here."

"When was the last time you did your monthly trade run?"

"Three weeks ago. Took Sarah and Louise with me. Was fixing to do another one next week."

"You notice anything out of the ordinary while you were at New Parker?"

"No, sir. Although . . ."

"Spit it out, son."

"Well, people were awfully anxious. Something about some War tech they scavenged from Amarillo. Doc Anderson described it as a kind of transponder. People were nervous 'bout it, although Doc said they might be able to communicate with other settlements around the country if they could get it working. It's not the first time they scavenged War tech, so I didn't give it much thought."

"Maybe so, but this was different, no?"

"Yes, sir."

"And you didn't think to mention it?"

Blake doesn't dare look at me, because I'm not too happy with him right now. I know he likes Doc Anderson because he's crazy smart and funny, and just plain likeable, if not a little strange. Doc probably wanted his new toy all hush-hush. But Carl's right: you're not supposed to keep these things to yourself. I'll definitely have a talk with Blake after our meeting.

The crowd's restless, and I know full well what the old-timers are thinking: they're thinking bad thoughts. I don't blame them either, because I'm thinking the same.

"All right, settle down," Carl says, and the crowd grows quiet. "I've already talked this over with the other councilmembers and we agree we need to send a patrol over to New Parker."

People start talking again, but Janet holds up a hand this time, and they fall silent. Our mayor is maybe five feet tall at the most, lean and in her late thirties, no children to account for, just a tiny thing, but strong and fair, which I respect.

"We're looking for four volunteers," she says. "You'll take the truck, see what's going on, and report back. That's all. But if something's wrong, you get back here right away. So . . ." She surveys the crowd. "Who's willing to go?"

It takes maybe a second or two of people looking around before hands get raised. I'd raise mine if it weren't for Little Mason and his sister. I'm not leaving them unprotected here. I look around for the other mechheads and see their hands ain't up either. They've also got family to protect. Going out in the new world is a young person's game. I've seen enough broken people and places for a lifetime.

Blake holds his hand high. I don't like it, but I can't say no. Blake's in charge of trade between settlements. If anyone knows New Parker, it's him.

Janet chooses Blake, along with Skip Harvey's two boys, Aaron and Kelsey, and Liz Morales. They're all around the same age, good kids, with decent heads on their shoulders, and they all know how to handle themselves, especially Liz, who's the best shot I've seen of anyone in our commune.

"Ya'll come with me," Carl says. "The rest of you are free to go home. We'll meet again as soon as we know something."

People break up into pockets and wander off. Unlike the last emergency town hall, this one has everyone on edge. Can't say I blame them.

Blake starts to head toward Carl and Janet, but I stop him.

"Not so fast. You and me gotta talk."

I T's A QUIET BREAKFAST at Sharon's. Little Mason and Maryann are busy eating their eggs and shredded potatoes while I ponder my talk with Blake. Of course I let him have it for keeping knowledge of the transponder to himself. Then I learned that he'd seen it. He described it as a cube about the size of a man's head, with smooth metal sides. Isaac-made, no doubt, judging from its simple shape. Isaac was always practical, even though he was a creative SOB. I should have stopped Blake from going to New Parker, and let someone else go. The whole reason we won the War was because we took down the network. Whatever transponders Isaac used were destroyed. We couldn't afford to keep the tech for ourselves because it would always be used against us. Those New Parkians were naïve to think otherwise. We've got shortwave for talking around the globe. They're crazy if they think some War tech communications module is gonna help them reach out to the rest of humanity.

Sharon's looking at me, her mug of tea cupped between her hands. Outside her small one-bedroom home, the sky is getting lighter. One of her roosters crows. The sun will be showing any minute. It's almost time to get to baling hay.

"Jedidiah, what's bothering you?"

"Ain't nothing," I say, moving around the spuds on my plate.

Sharon sets her cup down. "You're all skittish in front of the kids this morning. Is it about the town hall meeting? About Blake going to New Parker?"

"Just worried, that's all," I say, still playing with the potatoes. "Don't get me wrong. Blake knows how to handle himself. He's got his father's blood in his veins. But he's still a youngster. He ain't seen what I've seen."

Sharon's got brown hair going gray in the middle and lines around her eyes. Not even forty-two, but she lost her husband, and we're both a little more weathered than we should be.

When the kids finish, she shoos them off to get to studying. All the parents in town homeschool their children. Someday, when Potterville has grown, we'll scavenge enough books and build an honest-to-goodness school. Until then, we'll keep teaching the kids to read, write and do arithmetic like people have done for centuries.

Sharon refills her mug and gets me one too. Man, how I miss coffee.

I just let it out. "Been doing some thinking about ole Isaac lately."

"What sort of thinking?"

"There's a lot of hearsay he ain't dead, even though we killed him. And now with that transponder they found in the ruins in Amarillo, and Blake going to investigate . . ."

Sharon reaches across the table and takes my hand. Her skin is soft, but there are callouses, too, from working the field. "You worry about him a lot, don't you?"

"Sure I do. He's had it rough growing up. We're all he's got."

"You've had it rough, too, Jed, losing Suzy and—" She stops herself before saying my son's name. "Sorry, I didn't mean to bring it up."

I squeeze her hand. "That's all right. I've got you, Blake and the little ones to look after. At least I've got family."

She smiles at me, her eyes moist. Sharon has feelings for me, I know, but she's like my little sister. She needs to find another widower, someone smart like Carl.

"You're a good woman, Sharon."

She's got tears now. She's holding on to my hand, afraid to let it go as if we're caught in a storm. I'm afraid to let go, too. There's something awfully strong about the bonds between humans. No machine could ever understand that.

"Don't you worry," I tell her, sitting tall. "Ain't nothing going to happen to you and the kids as long as I'm around. And that's a solemn promise."

FIFTEEN-YEAR OLD SAM MCPHERSON ain't the sharpest tool in the shed, but he's a heck of a good ranch hand. We've got the sun scorching our backs as we tend to the only functioning hay baler in town.

I hear someone shouting. A girl is running through the field toward us, waving her hands back and forth. It's Elle, Carl's daughter. She's breathless by the time she reaches us, bent over and heaving, her dark hair clinging to the perspiration on her face.

"Easy, young lady," I say. "Catch your breath."

"It's—it's Blake," she says.

"What about him?"

"They radioed in and"—she sucks in another breath—"they said the whole town was quiet, like it was abandoned. Then Liz screamed and the radio went dead." She's almost in tears. "My dad asked for you."

I dig the tips of my fingers hard into the wrench I'm holding. I should have stopped Blake. Carl and Janet and the rest of the council were wrong about sending a volunteer patrol over to New Parker, especially with them inexperienced youngsters. Why didn't I stop them?

THERE'S NO TOWN HALL meeting this time, just the council and the lieutenants of Pottersquad, including Luke and Sheila. We're at the fix-it shop, where we machine parts from scavenged items hauled in from the ruins of Amarillo and our trading partners. It's more of an oversized shed than anything else, with a large workbench where nine of us are gathered around. On it is a paper hand-drawn map of New Parker. The settlement is approximately twice our size, the closest one to Amarillo. About three-hundred people live there, and they've got bullet-making down to a science. Beer brewing too. Not that it could help us now.

Carl follows the main avenue with a fat finger. There are buildings on either side, much like Potterville, except there's a larger town square in the middle, and the road branches in several places to a number of properties with scattered structures, some commercial or industrial from the looks of it. "They drove into town, that's for sure," he says. "Not sure where they parked, but Liz was on the brick after they got on foot."

"What did she say?" I ask.

"Said no one was around. Not a dang soul. They had to be downtown when the line went dead. Before we lost them, Liz said she saw it, mounted on a stake right in the center of town like some kind of scarecrow. It was buzzing, she said."

More like talking, as ole Isaac would have wanted it, but I keep that fact to myself. "Elle said she screamed."

Carl digs his fingers into his pudgy cheeks. His eyes are brimming, and we can all relate to the feeling.

Janet speaks up. "We need to take quick action. What resources can Pottersquad spare to go to New Parker? Ray?"

Ray Sarkisian, the Captain of Pottersquad, sighs like he's got the weight of the world on his shoulders, staring nowhere with big, puffy rings under his eyes. "I've got twenty good people at the ready. They know how to fight as well as the next person. As for vehicles, we've got our jeep, of course, and a couple of ATVs, but they're for short distance. We've got horses, too, but they're not conditioned for a fifty-mile ride. Plus, we don't know what we're dealing with. I gotta admit, I've never been as spooked as I am now. A whole town disappearing?"

"Who can we spare?" Janet asks.

"I'll go," I say, almost reflexively. Janet nods. No need explaining why.

Luke and Sheila volunteer, too, and Ray says he has a few more names in mind.

"One jeep isn't enough for everyone," Janet says. "The most she can hold is four, maybe five. The truck is gone, so what are we left with?"

No one says anything, because we've got diddly squat.

A sad look crosses Janet's face, reflecting our collective spirits. "We'll have to send the jeep then."

"We won't be able to patrol Potterville if you take the jeep," Ray says.

"So are you proposing we let those kids fend for themselves?"

Ray can't look Janet in the eye. It's a damned if you do, damned if you don't moment. But there is such a thing as priorities, and I for one ain't gonna let my nephew get stuck in some damned ghost town. It's got killing fields written all over it.

I clear my throat and propose something that hasn't seen the light of day in fifteen years, something I hoped we would never have to resort to, something we forbade ourselves from ever resurrecting. "I know a way we can solve both problems."

S HARON'S GOT THE KIDS with her, watching me as Sam McPherson and I pull open the old barn doors. They creak on rusty hinges, opening up to stale air and a dirt patch with a dusty blue tarp draped over what a passerby might assume is a tractor.

Sam's eyes grow big. "Is that it?"

I place a hand on his shoulder. I always pictured passing it along to Blake someday when I was old and the dangers of our past were forgotten.

Little Mason whistles. "That's big, Uncle Jed! Can I help?"

"Let's untie those knots." I point at the stakes where the eyelets of the tarp are secured by cord.

We each work on the four knots securing the tarpaulin. I've got two undone before either of the boys has theirs. I let them finish, though. Need to give them a chance to do their part.

"There!" Mason announces, crossing his arms, prouder than a peacock.

I step up on a table and pull on the big tarp. I can already smell what's underneath, the strong scent of valve grease working its way up. Even after all these years.

I hop down, dragging the tarp outside.

Stripes of sunlight from the barn windows strike the scraped gray torso of the mechanized exoskeleton standing nine feet tall. Eight-hundred pounds of pure, unadulterated mech. I grab a headband from its cradle on the workbench, dust it good and slip it over my forehead. I press the soft, rubbery button on the side. Hopefully it's still got juice.

The sound of a piston makes everyone but me jump back. I'm controlling the exo with my thoughts now. Just like riding a bicycle.

The heavy-duty ceramic-plated torso hinges open, and the flexible mechanical arms and legs expand to allow me to strap in. I step up on the knee guards bent outward at ninety degrees, pivot around, and sink one leg, then the other. I buckle in, then insert my arms. Chilled elastomesh wraps around my limbs. It'll keep me cool in the unforgiving sun. The actuators whir as I bend each arm and run through a calibrations check. Hot damn, it feels good to be sunk into my mech. I send command after command, forcing up the protective neck guard, checking my comm and onboard weapons system, wiggling the exaggerated, armored digits of each hand. I swivel and bend at the waist, servomotors humming their song, and reach for the zippered case containing my helmet. It's got the same powdered, gunmetal finish as the rest of my mech. It hooks neatly to the back of my neck flange. I'll use the heads-up display once we start going.

Little Mason jumps up and down, doing karate chops with his arms. "Waiyah!"

Sharon grabs a hold of his arm and shakes him. "Stop that! You respect your uncle, you hear?"

He stops, looks up at me like he's done something wrong, but then smiles when he sees me smiling. He'd make one helluva soldier. Hopefully, it'll never come to that. But still, he's got the warrior spirit.

"Now stand back." They move to the side as I send commands to my mech to move out. It's no different than lifting a leg. The exo boots stamp the ground with a heavy heel beat, and I think about that spine snapper in the sticks, and how good it would have been to cave in that eyeless sumbitch's antenna head.

Sam grabs my backpack with my bedroll, nine-millimeter handgun and spare mag, med kit, packaged dry food, and a portable transceiver with wired earpiece, and slips it into the exo's storage compartment in the back. He then follows my instructions to fill the water cylinder with a hose so I can sip from a straw built into my helmet when I need it. Can't rescue anyone if you're dying of thirst.

Sharon's got tears in her eyes. "You hurry back, Jedidiah, you hear me? And you bring our Blake home."

I give her a heartfelt smile and slip the helmet over my head.

The heads-up display shows Sheila and Luke's mechs about a half klick to the south. I activate the comm and tell them I'm on my way. I then break into a run. Pneumatic pistons cushion each stride. The exo can get up to twenty miles an hour without breaking a sweat.

"It's about damn time," Luke says. It's good hearing his voice through the comm. "Just like old times, huh?"

"Damned straight, bub."

Ahead, I see the dust cloud of my fellow mechheads. I clear my throat and speak into my comm. "Now let's show them New Parkians what the 509th Texan Brigade can do."

WE'RE MAKING GOOD TIME, although the day is waning. We've got maybe a couple hours of daylight left. Despite the built-in cooling, I'm perspiring. Can't have it too easy. Not like them Air Force boys from decades before, with their fancy air conditioning in their fixed winged aircraft. Man, do I miss having air support, though. What I wouldn't do for some eyes in the sky, telling us what's in store for us. All those satellites above, slowly falling to

Earth and doing nothing. No drones or planes. Heck, I'd be happy with a toy helicopter feeding us video.

We're running single file, Sheila in the lead, Luke second. I've got double duty, watching our six from the sides and rear. I'm the only one with an auto-feeder that still has ammo. Sheila's got an AR-50 automatic rifle, Luke an M4 carbine and shotgun. We'll scavenge for munitions if we have to. Hopefully, it won't come to that.

Left-right-left. Just like in the Corps.

My heads-up display blinks. It shows a trench across the broken road. More markers show up in my HUD, revealing a farmhouse, barn, stable and grain silo, judging by the shapes. The onboard database doesn't have much in terms of figuring out ordinary objects. It's all about the stuff that might kill us.

Minutes later, the HUD lights up the edge of town. The sun has dipped below the rows of dead cornhusks to the west. Strips of clouds ride above us, thicker bands along the east, and the occasional flicker of lightning. If I had a chance to stop and feel the air, I might tell if the storm is headed our way.

"Almost there," Sheila says, huffing from the exertion. Even though the exos are doing the majority of the work, we're still moving our limbs. She points northeast. "Get ready."

The HUD throws up a number of buildings concentrated along a well-traveled dirt road, lined with wheat fields to either side. We pass a combine harvester off to our left, with a partially-cleared field. The door is open. Someone must've left in a hurry.

Sheila signals for us to slow, and I drop to a light jog, then a march. Before we reach the outskirts of downtown, we come to a complete stop.

"Not a soul out," Luke says, removing his M4 from a jury-rigged mesh holster strapped to his right leg. "Creepy."

"This ain't our first rodeo," Sheila says.

I hear what she's saying, because that familiar wartime feeling washes over me, just like jumping into a lake with a weight belt on and nothing but your lungs and sheer willpower to get you out.

Sheila uses the built-in radio in her suit to contact the Pottersquad team back home. "Base, this is Charlie-Zulu, do you copy, over?" There's a lot of static and what sounds like a garbled voice on the other end. "Ray, is that you?" More static, then a persistent hiss. Sheila switches channels and tries again. "I'm not getting through," she tells us.

"Interference, you suppose?" Luke asks.

"Could be anything. Mind your sectors. Wedge formation."

We spread out, Sheila in the center and forward, me and Luke hanging back and to either side, creating a delta configuration for maximum coverage. I swivel every so many beats to make sure there aren't any threats behind us, then face front, and repeat the process. I hear my own breathing. It's like being stuck inside an empty water tank. I'm on high alert, filled with that same feeling I had fifteen years ago after Matheson finished his conversation with Isaac.

Downtown ain't too unlike ours, with a main dirt road splitting buildings left and right. There's a general store, fueling station, mill and machine shop. No cars or anything with wheels. Chickens are hunkered down inside a feed store, next to what looks like a large garage, with dual doors, all locked up. Then there's the roundabout in the town square, with a metal post in the center with what looks like old Christmas lights dangling from rungs running up. On top is what catches my attention: a cube mounted like a head on a pike. The cube is pure black, but looks like it's got an icy coating as it reflects the dying light of day. Fine, straight etching runs along the seams, spilling out faint, bluish light.

"You catching that?" Luke asks.

My comm picks up electronic chatter, machine talk. Pure gibberish to my human ears, but my mech's computer has identified it as a variant of Isaac talk. "Goddamned machine dialect. Where's it transmitting?"

Luke's exo shrugs.

"It's got to be communicating with a ground relay station," Sheila says. "Signal output is about good for a hundred klicks, and then it attenuates."

"Amarillo?"

"Probably. You've got your sonar tracking on, Jed?"

I'm pinging the crap out of everything around me, using echolocation like some kind of bat to try to find the townsfolk in the growing dark. "Not seeing anyone. Blake usually parks by one of two warehouses, depending on whether he's trading for dry goods or munitions."

"Luke, locate the buildings for us."

Luke's got a digital copy of Carl's New Parker map. He points south, then southwest. "Weapons depot is way over there, past the last building, the other warehouse a klick farther down the road. You think they're hiding out in one of them? I'm not picking up any heat signatures in the vicinity."

"We'll be systematic and search building to building," Sheila says. "Let's hump it out to the depot and see what's up."

"What do you want to do about this thing?" Luke motions to the humming transponder.

I swear the blue light in the cube flickers bright for a second, as if saying, "I see you, bub."

I volunteer my opinion. "I say we take it out."

Sheila agrees. "Luke, do the honor, but do it quietly."

Luke reaches up as high as he can with the arms of his suit. He grabs the metal pole and gives it a good shake. It takes maybe thirty seconds before the cube loosens enough to tumble to the ground. A thump with his exo boot puts it out of its misery.

Sheila nods her approval. "Switch formation to single element. I'll lead; Jed, you take up the rear."

We head out, single file.

Total darkness falls, and there's not a single light in any direction. My helmet automatically switches to night vision. We're quiet now. My audio picks up my breathing and our heavy steps, but nothing else. Can't conceal our movement, not with this much weight.

We crunch through dead grass and wade through brush and stalks, making a beeline for the warehouse, rather than going the long way using the roads. The building's got cinderblock walls and an A-frame cladded metal roof. Good, solid construction. It's big, about fifteen-thousand square feet by my estimate.

There's a large barnyard door in the center, paned windows around the sides, protected by rebar cages and painted black, and a metal side door. It's an oddity compared to anything we have in Potterville, where we leave doors and windows unlocked. People feel safe in our town, and Pottersquad makes sure of it. Can't say the same for this place.

Fifty feet from the warehouse Sheila has us halt. I sip some water and wait. She orders us to fan out to cover all angles of approach. I'm covering the side door, gunner arm raised, HUD in targeting mode.

"I'm picking up something mechanical from inside," she says in a low voice. "It's chattering away."

"Same dialect as before," I add. "Bet you five chits it's trying to talk to our friend in town. Good thing we destroyed that thing."

"Whatever it is, stay sharp. We're going through the barn door in tactical formation. Jed, you've got the firepower. Take the lead."

I step to the front of our column and close the gap to the warehouse. Floodlights kick on and I freeze, temporarily blinded. My helmet switches to the visible spectrum and I see the motion-sensor floodlight mounted underneath the eave. My heart's racing a hundred miles an hour.

I grab hold of the bracketed handle to the barnyard door. I give it a slight tug. It's locked. Actuators kick in and redirect power to my forearm. "Going in," I whisper.

I pull hard.

There's a groan, then a snap, followed by a sudden give as the door squeals open to my left. My HUD orients to the massive yawn of dark, making out details in shades of amber. I don't have but a second before I see something big, real big, and it ain't human.

Luke's voice squawks in my comm. "Holy mother of God!"

Spindly legs retract into a flying saucer mass the size of a small bulldozer, sensors ringed around its body like eyes. Antennas writhe back and forth, along with whiplike feelers on its legs. I can't tell what's metal and what's not, because the whole crablike apparatus seems to flex like a great big breathing horror. But it's the razor-sharp talons that have my full attention. I hear them clank against the concrete slab of the floor. They can only be made for one thing: ripping people apart.

I fire a burst of hoo-yahs dead center.

The skin deforms, like denting an old pickup. The thing reflexively draws most of its limbs into its center, but lashes out with one of its legs, making contact with my mech. I stagger to the side, vibration running throughout my armor. My exo's stabilizers kick in, preventing me from losing my balance. No damage from what I can tell.

I catch the muzzle flash from Sheila's .50 cal. The blast shatters a piece of the crab's armor, knocking it back temporarily. It's got a built-in stabilizing mechanism too, because instead of dropping back, it launches forward, as if unharmed.

Sheila shrieks as the crab crashes into her. She tumbles backward, knocking into Luke, tipping him sideways. The thing barrels on, galloping into the open. It goes maybe ten strides before skidding to a halt, sending weeds and dirt flying. My HUD can't identify the sumbitch. I need my targeting system to find its power source so we can take it out.

Looks like it's going to be the hard way.

"Hang on!" I yell into my comm.

I send a command to my left forearm and my twelve-inch, carbon-steel combat knife springs out as I rush the thing. I fire three-round bursts, targeting joints and sockets. I need to disable its ability to balance. It raises two of its eight legs in a defensive posture, pawing the air like a black widow ready to strike. Its underbelly is exposed, black plates showing up bright and nasty under spotlights, spread apart to reveal sickly black skin.

The claws come down full force, but not before I rip into the flexible metal skin of its belly. The strike knocks me to my knees with a great shudder. I'm yanking with my knife, ripping that metal, hoping to damage something big. Black fluid squirts onto the ground, as if I've severed an artery. But it ain't blood, because it ain't alive.

The thing tries to whip me around as Luke and Sheila blast it with almighty firepower. I'm stuck on something hard in its belly. It's jumping like a bucking bronco, trying to dislodge me. I'm still on my knees, getting thrashed about and pounded into the ground. My kneepads absorb the shock, but my poor arm feels like it's about to get ripped out of its socket.

With my free arm I start punching up.

Whap, whap, whap.

I'm hitting its protective plates. They flex in, then out. What in God's name is this thing made of?

Two of its side legs sag suddenly, tilting its mass right. I grab hold of the claw of the sagging leg and pull. Servomotors wheeze as I strain. A second later, there's a loud pop and the leg is yanked free from its socket, like ripping a claw from a lobster.

From above, there's a godawful judder of metal on metal, again and again. Luke or Sheila's beating the crap out of the thing. It gives me a chance to shift power to my knife arm. With everything I've got, I pull sideways. The plates start popping out as I rip a gash into the crab bastard and then drive inward, slashing through delicate instruments. The whole thing shivers like mad. By the time I've ripped free, it falls to the side, clawing itself, dragging its carcass in a large sweeping circle. I stand back and aim my firing arm, just in case. My HUD picks up electric hissing of communication in its Isaac dialect, but it sounds more like the death throes of agony.

And then it's really dead.

No more crazy clacking or whining of pistons or actuators. It's a lump of nothingness, spilling the last of its coolant blood onto the thirsty earth.

Sheila tips her rifle down, and Luke drops a large length of piping that he had ripped from the building's exterior to use like a baseball bat on our crab fellow. We sound like a bunch of bears breathing.

"You want to tell me what the hell that was?" Luke says.

My HUD still has nothing to show. If ole Isaac made the thing, it's new to me.

I give one of its sprawled-out limbs a kick. Still dead. "Those eyes give me the creeps."

"They're not eyes," Sheila says. "They're acoustical sensors. It saw by sound and vibration."

"Are you kidding me?"

"One thing we can be sure of: it was attracted to something in that warehouse. Something alive."

"Blake!" I head for the open door.

"Jed, wait up!" Sheila says, but I ain't listening.

I've got my combat knife and all two-hundred-ninety-four remaining hoo-yahs ready for any other terror waiting to ambush us inside. I'll kill every crab monster that gets in the way of finding my nephew and the other kids.

I switch to ground-penetrating radar and ping the hell out of the place. Walls and machinery answer back with their echoes. There are wooden crates and pallets everywhere, along with workbenches, shelves, 3D printers and rows of empty casings, a cache of bullets and a few metal lower receivers for automatic weapons. No humans. I ping the floor next as I walk across the concrete slab. Something's below us, like a basement, but I can't see. Some kind of shielding blocks me.

"Jed, over here," Luke says from the other side of a conveyor belt. "I'm tracking a heat signature under this grating. Three distinct signatures."

Three, not four? My heart beats something crazy in anticipation as Luke grabs the grating and tries to yank it free. Its starts to flex, then a rivet snaps, followed by the whole thing.

There's a scream. A human scream.

Sheila is already getting out of her exo, unbuckling her harness. Her helmet is off, and her hair is a mess, matted to her sweaty forehead. "Liz, is that you?"

"Sheila! Oh, my God!"

It's Liz Morales for sure, and my heart leaps from my chest. Only three signatures, I keep thinking.

A flashlight clicks on, and I see Liz scramble up a staircase into Sheila's arms. She's sobbing. I'm getting out of my exoskeleton, too, but not before I tell Luke to stand guard.

Aaron Harvey comes up next, followed by his brother, Kelsey, who's holding the flashlight. They're quivering like leaves, scared out of their blanking minds.

Three signatures.

I jump down from my mech, hop the conveyor belt and rush over to the kids. "Where's Blake?"

Aaron looks at me, then drops his head. Kelsey grabs hold of Sheila and Liz and starts crying too.

I take Aaron by the shoulders and give him a shake. "Where's my nephew?" He won't look up. I shake him again. "Where's Blake, goddammit?"

He looks at me, and it's hard to see with just the spotlight on outside, but I can tell everything's gone to hell. "They took him," he finally manages to say.

"Who's 'they'?"

He's got that thousand-yard stare I've seen soldiers get the first time they see someone get killed.

I let off the gas just a little. No sense throttling the answer out of him. "It'll be okay, son. Now tell me what happened."

I'M CROUCHED BY WHERE Aaron is sitting on the ground outside, listening to him talk. Above us the mosquitos and moths are going crazy in the spotlight, and the air is thick and humid. There's a rumble of thunder in the distance. Luke has our six, standing guard a few feet away in his mech. Kelsey is by himself, arms crossed, tapping his foot nervously.

"Where did you see it happen?" I ask Aaron.

"Right outside this big brick building, clear on the other side of town," he says. "Blake said it's where Doc Anderson has his shop."

"Why did you go there?"

"Because everyone was missing. The whole town. Like vanished. Blake thought if anyone stuck around, it would be Doc. So we went to Doc's. We heard these sounds, like scraping, and . . ." Aaron's breathing hard. He looks at Sheila, who's got Liz leaning her head against her shoulder.

"Keep going," I say. "What happened?"

"Blake insisted on checking it out. We told him not to look in the window, but he did. Then the window shattered, and they grabbed him."

"Who grabbed him?"

Aaron shakes his head, eyes getting all shiny, about to weep. "It was a man, but not a man." He's gasping for air. I let him go through the motions. A few seconds later, he gets control of his breathing. "Something was wrong with his face. There was something clamped over his head. I—I can't . . ."

All I'm thinking about now is getting to Blake. Even if he's gone and gotten himself killed. I'll never forgive myself if I don't see him with my own eyes.

Damn that boy for having guts. And for being foolish, too.

I get to my feet, dust my jeans, and help Aaron to a standing position.

"We need to gear up," Sheila says. "Get a move on."

I remember seeing weapon parts inside the warehouse, and bullet casings. Maybe we can scavenge some munitions.

I turn to Aaron. "Where's your truck?"

"Just up the road."

"You can either stay here and wait for us, or come with. Your decision."

Aaron's face gets serious, his weepy eyes steely now. "No way. We're going with you. I can fight."

I size him up. He's on the skinny side, six feet and change, but determined. Liz nods, willing to go as well, and from the corner of my eye I see Kelsey nodding, too.

"Right," I say. "Let's get to it."

W E MANAGED TO PUT the upper and lower receivers together to make two AR-15 rifles. They're decent quality, a combination of machined and 3D-printed metal alloy parts. Those bullets I saw turned out to be forty-five-mil. Liz and Kelsey helped fill the twenty-round magazines while I showed Aaron how to use my .45. Liz already knew how to use an AR-15. That left Kelsey, who got a quick lesson.

"Remember," I say, "don't aim at anything you don't plan to shoot."

Kelsey swallows, but he gets it.

"Now, because it's dark, we're going to take the lead with our mechs. You kids follow us in the truck, but keep them headlights off. Fog lamps only. Kelsey, you drive. Aaron and Liz, get in the bed of the truck. You're our rearguard, so stay alert. Ya'll with me?"

They give a round of nods, and we're on the road, three mechs in front, side-by-side, phalanx style, Kelsey and the others behind us in their truck. The transceiver they have with them hisses static just like our built-ins, except we're able to talk among ourselves at this short distance. We're in the dark for long-range talking, unable to communicate with Potterville. Janet and the others must be beside themselves worrying about us. Whatever cut off the town's communication is probably jamming us as well.

Sheila has us at a light infantry jog. There weren't any .50 caliber rounds for her to scavenge, and unfortunately we had no time to make any, although the warehouse was a slam-dunk for machining ammunition with all its hardware. Luke lucked out, though, able to use the same .45 rounds for his M4, so he's stocked and locked.

The brick building is larger than I pictured. Maybe because it's two stories and long as heck—seriously, like a city block. There are dirty, paned windows on both levels, wrapping around the entire length. A small dirt road is all that leads to it, branched off from the main avenue. Mesquite shrubs, junipers and cottonwoods jump up from the short-grass prairie around it, along with the remnants of a corn field. Who the heck thought of building this son-of-a-gun over here, and for what purpose?

We slow to a walk.

"All dark and quiet," Luke says into the comm.

Sheila motions in front of her with her rifle. "Let's break up and do a three-sixty of the exterior. Luke, left flank, Jed, right."

"Rodge on that."

I radio Kelsey. "Hey, Kelse, hang back a little. We're going to check things out. Tell Liz and Aaron what's happening and to listen for trouble. You catch wind of anything, you holler, ya hear?"

"Sure, sure," he says, sounding all nervous. Got to hand it to him for toughing it out.

I let my squad know I'm switching to sonar.

The three-sixty takes five minutes. Ain't nothing but empty rooms from what I could tell, perhaps a communal bathroom, as if this were an old apartment building, or hostel. I'm back by the front, where shattered glass litters the ground. The building entrance is too small for our exos to fit through. That means we need to downsize, and downsizing ain't good when you're in the middle of the sticks with three-hundred people missing.

"I'm picking up residual heat on the first level," Sheila says.

"Something's moving," Luke says. "I'm boosting my radar."

"Speak to me, Luke."

"Single figure, male I'm guessing. He's headed—hang on a sec."

"Luke?"

"He just disappeared!"

"Did he stop moving perhaps?"

"No, I mean he disappeared. There's a subterranean level, so he could have gone down there."

Could it be Blake, running scared? The idea doesn't fit in with the facts. Aaron swore up and down Blake was taken. Right through that window.

"I'm going in," I announce. I send a series of commands to my exo to release me.

Sheila is quick to protest. "Jed, we don't know anything about what's waiting for us inside. You saw what happened at the warehouse."

"My nephew is in there. You stay put with Luke and let me scout ahead."

Sheila starts to say something else, but I've got my helmet off and I'm un-buckling my harness. I grab a flashlight from the suit backpack, along with my shotgun, nine-mil and portable radio. There's a buzz of crickets from the trees, but no sound coming from the building. Liz is out of the truck with her rifle and her flashlight, Aaron too.

"Where do you think you're going?"

"With you," Liz says.

I don't have time to argue. "Fine. Swap guns with Luke. You'll want the carbine for close quarters. Same thing with you, Aaron; exchange guns with your brother. Let's move!"

I hook the radio earpiece to my ear and tune into our channel while the kids hustle. "Mike check, one-two," I transmit.

"Reading you loud and clear," Sheila says back.

I give Liz a ten-second tutorial on using her flashlight in tandem with the carbine as we approach the building, a tactical maneuver for targeting in the dark. She's a quick study, the type of person that only needs to be told once.

"Get that door for me, will ya?" I say into my mike.

Luke steps over, metal boots thumping the ground. His actuators whine as he leans forward and grabs the outside door by the handle. A big ole tug shears the lock. I duck under his arm and head in, followed by the kids.

We're up a small stairwell, through another door and into a long hallway with doors on either side. We don't have sonar, radar or infrared to help us in here, just our God-given eyes. Hopefully Luke and Sheila can watch out for us.

"Stay close," I whisper as I sneak along the corridor. Lots of dust in here and a moldy smell that gets worse by the second. There's a bunch of footprints in the dusty old vinyl floor, the fresher ones leading in the direction we're headed.

We slow by the community bathroom. I shine my light inside and catch several rats scurrying under one of the stalls. I bend down to take a peek. The toilets are cracked porcelain with rust stains and the smell of century-old piss. Nothing to see other than bad plumbing.

When we get to the end of the hall, we come to an open door to one of the rooms, and a staircase going down. There's all kinds of lab equipment set up, scopes and what not, much of it battered looking, probably scavenged, but all looking like it was used recently. Tons of books are stacked up high on tables. Someone's been doing research.

I point down the stairwell. The kids get the picture: we're going below-ground. Liz's eyes are big. She just survived being stuck under a slab of concrete. "It'll be okay," I whisper. I wish somebody would convince me the same. I speak low into my mike to let Luke, Sheila and Kelsey know what we're about to do.

I give the kids a hand signal: watch your tail.

The stairwell is broken up into two sections, zigging one way then the other. At the bottom, there's a heavy metal door. Liz whispers from behind. "What's that sound?"

It's the hum of a generator, mixed with the hiss of steam and the clunking of metal. Machinery. Something big's going on here.

"Let's find out," I say. I count down from three, pray nothing ghoulish is waiting to get us, and pull it open. It squeals something terrible to show us a long stretch of dark.

As soon as we step into the long hallway, LED lights click on overhead. I freeze for a moment, but see nothing but concrete floor and walls plastered with yellowing subway tiles. At the end is a single door with a safety glass window, and light beyond it. There's a video camera above it, pointed our way, and one above us, facing the other direction, with a motion sensor. No point going low and slow.

I take the lead, and run toward the door with my gun aimed. The kids are on my heels, huffing behind me. The unnatural smell of drain cleaner seeps into my nostrils, some kind of ammonia scent, and gets real strong when we reach the door. I don't even bother peeking inside. I yank on the lever handle, sweat pouring from my brow, and pull with my free hand. It's godawful heavy, but the door budges.

The room balloons out into a large bay filled with dozens of beds that remind me of one of those makeshift hospitals you'd find in a warzone, except with no privacy curtains. Each bed's hooked up to a bundle of black wiring hanging from an IV pole that snakes into the back to a large machine like an octopus, bundling all those wires into a trunk of cabling that feeds into a bank of computers. My eyes fall upon the six beds with bodies. They're dressed in scrubs with an assortment of tubes and wires running to IVs and monitors. They have black shells over their scalps, shiny like beetles, with tiny feelers springing out and sunk into their temples, wrapped around their throats and plunged into their eye sockets. The ammonia smell masks urine and other foul odors, making me want to gag.

A skinny man stands in the back with a shaved head, in a white lab coat stained with blood and dirt. He's got black metal discs where his eyes should be and small feelers wrapped around to the back. They're like the antennas we saw on that crab thing at the warehouse, moving like they're trying to pick up a signal.

I point my gun downrange, ready to drop this sorry sack if he breathes wrong. I start toward him. The kids don't seem to know how to process the scene, but they follow me.

"Hey there, bub, want to tell me what's going on here?"

The bedding on most of the empty beds is stained yellow and brown, probably from bodily wastes, and dark-red and ocher around the head area from blood and machine fluids. Why are there only six people left? What happened to the rest? What happened to Blake?

"It's too late," the man says. His voice ain't right. It's hollow and sad and downright not the natural sound a man should be making. I spot a couple of the feelers' tails snaked around his throat.

I click on my mike so Sheila and Luke can listen in. The feelers around his throat are vibrating, like a spider's leg on its web. "Too late for what?" I ask.

"For all of us."

The words send chills up my spine. "How about we back up and start with your name, mister? What's this all about, and what's your role in it?"

He shakes his head, like he's tortured and fighting with himself. "I'm Dr. Anderson," he says. "My role?" He begins to laugh. "Oh God, don't ask me that. Don't ask me to tell you. Please."

"I'm not asking, and my friend here"—I emphasize the gun—"says you've got a few seconds before I put a round in your left thigh. So, how about it? What's going on here, Doc? What did you do to these people?"

He turns his black mirrored lenses toward the six bodies. I'm close enough now to see there are two women and four men lying on their stained beds. The monitors show their vitals. Half are flat-lined, the others alive.

"He told me to do it," Doc says. "Oh God, he made me do it!"

"You better start explaining real fast. What did you do to these people?"

"Not me. It wasn't me. It was him! He's in my head. He's everywhere!" Doc shudders something awful. He's all twisted up, invaded by the contraption dug into his skull.

I'm close enough now to check the bodies. Of the two males still breathing, one is beefy. A wave of nausea and relief hit me at once.

"Blake!" Liz blurts out and rushes over. Aaron is right behind her.

I try to caution her to stand back, but the voice gets squeezed out of my throat. My Blake is alive! But he's . . .

"What are those things around their heads?" I ask Doc. "How do we get them off?"

Doc's mirrored eyes turn back to me. "You can't take them off. They're keeping them alive. If you try to surgically remove the BCIs, the host will die."

"You better help me get my nephew out of this, or I'll start making your life real unpleasant, you hear?"

"I"—he grits his teeth for a sec—"can't."

"Can't or won't?"

"He won't let me! Don't you understand?"

"I'm giving you a count of three." I point my gun at his quad. "Three . . . two . . ."

"I can't just do what you want. I—"

An earsplitting blast sounds as I pull the trigger. Doc cries out and falls to his knees.

Liz screams at me. "What are you doing?"

I ignore her. I haul Doc to his good leg and place the barrel of the gun to his ribcage. "I'll say this one more time. Are you going to help my nephew?"

Doc is panting, and whatever puppet strings have him at bay are released momentarily. "Yes, but please don't kill me."

I jab the metal into his side. "Then you better make it quick."

Doc limps over to Blake, removes the IV line from his arm, and pulls away the top part of his scrubs to get to the electrodes on his chest. All the while, the feelers on the thing clamped over Blake's head wriggle, like they're alive.

"What was Isaac planning on doing with my nephew? What did he promise you in return?"

Doc's hands are shaking and his breathing is raspy. He's fighting to stay in control of his body as blood starts to pool at his feet.

I move the barrel of the gun to the side of his head. "Answer me!"

"I thought we could find a technological solution to our problems," he says between rapid breaths, "maybe find a way to rebuild our community and connect to others out there. We scavenged the Amarillo ruins, looking for War tech. We figured Isaac was destroyed, so there was nothing to worry about."

"Nothing to worry about?" I'm ready to rip those black discs out of his eye sockets. What did my nephew see in him? Why did he and the rest of New Parker put their trust in this demented creature?

"It was naïve, I agree," Doc says quickly, carefully working his fingers around Blake's jawline and up to the feelers. They're like root tendrils, testing Doc's skin like they're trying to find new earth to dig into. The pool of blood around his feet is getting larger. He might bleed out. "Our town's patrollers found a War-era transponder in Amarillo. My assistant James and I figured out how to make it work. We took apart the upper chassis of a DC-60 heavy duty robot that had been scavenged a while back. DCs were androids the military used on the frontlines before the War."

"I know this. You're wasting my time."

With a nudge of my gun, he speeds up. "James and I took the beast apart until we found the communications module. We hooked it up to a computer, then used it, along with the transponder, to reverse engineer Isaac's compromised comm network. If we could find anyone else out there with the right tech, then we could see if there were any cities—real, functioning cities."

"But you found Isaac instead."

Doc turns Blake's head to the side. "He tricked us. I thought I was talking to a fellow woman scientist in Toronto, but it was him. She gave me specific instructions on building a brain-computer interface with optics that would allow me to see machine chatter. It was more advanced than anything we knew. Leftover tech from Isaac's war factory. It was supposed to give me 'the sight,' but instead . . ."

"Instead it took yours and opened a whole can of worms." *Dumb as smart,* my Daddy used to say.

"What are you doing to him?" Liz asks.

Doc tugs on one of the small whips dug into Blake's left temple. It pops free, along with a small dribble of blood, and he places a square of gauze over it. "Severing command and control. Just have one more to go. Hold here and apply pressure while I get the other one."

Liz presses down with her fingers as Doc angle's Blake's head the other way.

"What do you mean 'command and control'?" I ask.

Doc lightly touches each of the whips, as if testing for the right one. Whatever pain he's in, he's found the off switch. It ain't natural. His right hand starts trembling and he has to clamp his left over it to steady himself. "Human-machine hybridization. The creation of the first hybrid army, designed for the express purpose of seeking out and destroying other humans. An extermination force."

Doc's words swirl in my brain. I think of Mason and Maryann back home, and all the good people of Potterville.

"The machines can't do it themselves," Doc continues, biting into his bottom lip and clamping down harder on his rogue wrist. "Their network was broken when Isaac was destroyed, and they lacked strong AI to serve a leadership role. So the fragments of Isaac's War sought a new source, something that could create a singularity."

"Are we dealing with Isaac or something else?"

"It's more like Isaac 2.0." Doc lets go of his wrist. It's shaking a little, but not all crazy like before. He finds the whip to unplug. "I don't know what's going to happen when I pull this. I'm seeing a lot of chatter. Bad, bad, bad."

"What happened to the three-hundred people in this town? Where did they all disappear to?"

Doc shakes his head. He doesn't want to answer me.

Sheila speaks into my comm. "Jed, do you copy?"

"I'm in the middle of something. What's up?"

"There's a lot of machine chatter. I'm picking up an inbound signal. I need you topside."

"We'll be up in a few."

"You need to get up here now!"

Damn it. I grab Doc's shoulder and shove my barrel hard against his ribs. "Where is everyone?"

"Half the townspeople were exterminated. They're burned in a mass grave. About a quarter couldn't integrate with the new hardware, so they didn't make it either. The other quarter got their retrofits. This here is the last batch."

"Where did these retrofits go?" His trembling stops, so I let go of his wrist.

Doc pinches the whip with one hand and readies a piece of gauze with the other. "He only tells me what he wants me to know. He's in my head all the time. He sees what I see, hears what I hear, understand?"

This new Isaac doesn't have the means to annihilate us as a species . . . yet. Bottom line: we can't let the body find the head. If we do, it's game over. "You have to know something," I say.

"I assume the Mercury units are marching with the retrofits. Amarillo, I'd guess. That's where the signal's originating from. They left yesterday morning. As for the other machines, who knows? When this last batch of retrofits is ready, they'll follow the trail of the others. They'll have no choice."

"Well, we're about to be one less slave, aren't we?"

Doc pulls the last whip free from Blake's temple.

The two other living hybrids snap upright on their beds, dragging their wires and tubes with them. They're on their feet, the heads and tops of their faces hidden by the black beetle things clamped over them. The suddenness of their movement startles the bejesus out of all of us. The taller one, built like a forward tackle of a pro football team, grabs hold of the IV pole and raises it like a baseball bat over Liz. It don't take but a moment to set my gun hip level and squeeze off a round. Football guy staggers back from the blow, tipping to the side with the IV pole. A second bullet to the throat puts him down for good.

The woman, though, clamps on to Aaron, clawing at his face.

Liz snags her M4 from the ground and fires a burst at the woman's lower leg. The bullets puncture her calf, sending blood shooting from some artery. It slows her down some. She's climbed her way onto Aaron's back, scraping her nails into his neck and face, drawing blood, ignoring pain no person could ever ignore. Isaac's found a way to shut off the hurt.

Aaron, being a tall boy, finds purchase somewhere on her arm, spins the both of them, and flings her off. She's turned around for only a second. By the time she turns back for another go at it, Liz finishes her off with a spray of bullets to the chest. The deafening *pop, pop, pop*, lingers in my head, giving my eardrums a good ringing.

Liz is breathing hard, body all tense. Poor Aaron's face is all scraped to hell, with trickles of blood in several places, but he ain't hurt bad, thank goodness. He just got a lesson in survival, just as all of us got a lesson in what this new Isaac is capable of. I turn to Doc, ready to rip him a new one for being the one responsible for all of this, but he's leaning heavily against one of the beds, pale faced and sweating.

Sheila speaks into my earpiece urgently, her voice crackly from interference. "Jed, head topside right now! I'm picking up a pretty big signature here."

"Roger that," I radio back. I grab a fistful of Doc's lab coat. "You're coming with us."

"They can track him, can't they?" Aaron asks.

The boy's got a point. If we take Doc, they'll paint a target, and we'll all be doomed. If we don't, we might not be able to help Blake.

"Can you turn off that link of yours?"

Doc shakes his head. He's having trouble standing upright, and there's a mess of blood below his shoes. He ain't going to make it either way. Better to put him out of his misery than to give Isaac another chance to work against us.

Doc seems to sense what I'm about to do. "It's okay. I'm ready."

"Sorry, bub." I point my gun at his head.

"Don't!" Liz cries, but she's too late. A single shot puts Doc down for good. Liz looks at me. "Haven't we done enough killing?"

"It was necessary. Now let's get out of here."

Aaron helps me get Blake off the table and into a fireman's carry while Liz takes the lead. I whisper a prayer for the dead.

I talk into my mike as I hustle behind Aaron. "We've got our package. Whadya got?"

"Don't know, Jed," Sheila says. "But you better hurry your ass. We've got a shitload of activity."

"Hump it out!" I shout at Liz and Aaron, moving as fast as I can with Blake's body bouncing over my back.

By the time we're topside, my legs and lungs are screaming and my clothes are soaked through with sweat. Sheila's shouting at us to get going. I hand Blake off to Liz and Aaron, who get him loaded up in the bed of the truck. I dash over to my mech while Kelsey powers up the truck.

I climb aboard my exo and slip on my headband just as Luke shouts into our comms.

"We've got inbounds! Rollers!"

I hear them coming just as I send commands to my mech to get the show on the road. It sounds like a swarm of bowling balls heading for us, but rollers aren't just mindless spheres of metal. They hunt by vibration and heat, each about the size of a watermelon, and carry a nasty payload of liquid that explodes when it makes contact with air.

Sheila and Luke open fire with the *rat-tat-tat* of metal on metal, causing a chain-reaction of explosions, taking out the entire cluster of rollers. My mech shudders from the blasts and my heat sensors register the fireball.

My HUD floods with a new set of inbound bogies, coming the opposite direction from the first wave. The column of rollers bounces down the incline to the east, flattening dead corn stalks. I fire a burst of hoo-yahs. The balls scatter, but I manage to tag one, and it blows, sending up an eruption of earth and dried husks. The ones that came for Luke and Sheila probably didn't have the maneuvering room, so they all took each other out. Now we've got multiple targets. *Shit, shit, shit!*

Luke fires, Sheila too. Even Liz. It's the fight of our lives.

The balls have momentum, but they can change direction too. The rollers explode as they're hit, like an enemy position struck by continuous bombardment, but there are too many for us to take out.

"Fall back!" Sheila shouts.

"Kelsey, get that truck out of here," I tell the kid through my comm. "Head north, back toward the main road."

"Copy that," Kelsey says, popping the truck into gear.

We concentrate our firepower on the frontline of inbounds to give Kelsey lead time with the truck. The detonations rock the ground around us.

As soon as the truck clears, Sheila signals us to fall back.

We break into a run. Rollers can outpace a human on a smooth surface any day, but on uneven ground, they have to use integrated coils to help them spring-and-roll to keep up. Compared to our mechs, they're no match.

As soon as we hit the main road, we catch up to the truck, putting good distance between us and the rollers. The truck's got its high beams cutting through the dark. When we hit downtown, my HUD flashes red. Something's very wrong with one of the buildings up ahead.

"Kelsey, stop the truck!" I shout.

Kelsey slows to a stop near the center of town.

"What the hell is that?" Luke asks. He's asking about the source of the signal, the garage with the double doors next to where the chickens were roosting for the night.

There's a groan of metal, followed by the splintering of roof shingles. The whole structure bursts apart a moment later, sending wood, glass and siding everywhere. A jagged machine leg smashes through the remaining metalwork of the garage doors, landing a satellite dish-sized claw on the street with a heavy thump. Pistons whine and the top of the machine rises through the ruins. It's outfitted with armor plates shielding a turret in the center that's pivoting toward us.

"Shambler!" Sheila shouts.

My HUD IDs the thing. It's a slow-moving, heavy-duty walker tank with four legs. It ain't fast 'cause it don't need to be. It just needs to aim and fire. It appears surreal through my amber-colored night vision, ugly and blocky, but it wasn't built for its looks.

"I'll draw its fire away from the truck," I say. "Sheila, find another way out of here!"

I run to the left of the roundabout. I'm waving at the shambler, trying to grab its attention as I head toward it. As I hoped, the turret tracks me. I try to keep one step ahead of the cannon, running at full throttle with my carbon-steel blade ready and auto-feeder locked and loaded. I'm not prepared to die, even though it seems that's what I'm looking for.

The shambler fires its cannon. A shell whizzes by, blowing the building behind me to smithereens. I'm struck with chunks of brick and metal and whatever else it's made out of.

"Jed, move your ass!" Sheila screams through my comm.

"I'm moving!"

My HUD registers a reload of ammunition. I zig to the right, crashing into the wall of the general store just as another shell fires past me. A wallop of an explosion sounds, sending a vibration through my exo armor as I shatter glass and rip apart clapboards with my momentum.

I'm less than fifty feet and closing. My HUD indicates another reload. The thing is in the street now, all four legs fixed while the turret moves about its center of mass. It's got to be twenty feet tall and plated out the wazoo with antiaircraft-grade armor. My only option is to try to tip it over.

I run full tilt, pushing my legs and actuators to their capacity. The motors scream to keep up with my computer-aided movements. An alarm screeches in my HUD, telling me the Shambler's targeting system has me locked in. I unload a torrent of hoo-yahs at its sensor array. They ricochet harmlessly off the armor, but it's the heat signature I'm after. For an instant, the targeting system loses me. Then it locks on again. I duck below the barrel and crash into the tank's housing as it fires its cannon. The combination of recoil and my impact deflect me wide, like I just ran into a wall headfirst, and a burst of pain wracks my skull. My exo's built-in stabilizers keep me from hitting dirt, even though the wind has been knocked out of me. The groaning of the shambler's massive hulk filters into my external microphone as the tank legs attempt to right themselves. It staggers back, or attempts to, but unlike the claw monster, it's got no arms. One leg twists under the strain, then the other, and the whole thing topples. Its turret rips through a machine shop, landing the beast smackdab in the middle of the store, annihilating everything in its wake, and sending up a cloud of dust and debris.

"Whoa, way to smoke him!" Luke calls into the comm.

"He's down, not out," I say, trying to regain my wits, head still aching like I'd ridden a bull at a rodeo. The shambler starts to rise from the store, tilting it upright. It's the self-leveling pistons in its sidewall, and judging by the rate it's pushing, I'd say we've got under a minute before T-rex is back in commission.

Luke and Sheila run toward me, the kids right behind them in their truck. "I thought I told you to head out," I say.

"There was no time to figure out another route," Sheila says, huffing through her comm. "We've got rollers inbound. Sixty seconds to contact!"

My HUD picks them up, swarming toward us like the black plague. Sheila catches up to me, and we start running like crazy. I'm not happy we can't put this shambler out of its misery, but with the rollers after us, there's no time.

We outpace the rolling tide of death, leaving the possessed ghost town of New Parker behind us.

Within the hour, we ease into a jog. Something's wrong with the alignment of my chassis, forcing my actuators to work double-time to keep me moving in a straight line. Still, it's good enough to make it back to Potterville. Above us, the clouds split apart, and thirty minutes later, the sky lightens, telling us dawn is coming. All the while, Sheila is transmitting to Potterville, and I'm hoping to God Isaac ain't listening.

Our radio finally receives a reply from a frantic and much-relieved Carl, and we all break into cheer.

"Oh, thank the Lord!" he says. "I thought ya'll were dead."

"We're a lot harder to kill than you think," Sheila says, and we all give in to a much-needed round of laughter.

When the laughing dies off, Carl asks, "What happened out there?"

"Tell you all about it when we get home. Make sure you assemble just the leadership. Have them gather at the fix-it shop. We'll do a town hall meeting after."

"Everyone's worried about you. I can't just hide it from them."

"Carl, do as I say. Please. We need to see Dr. Roberts pronto. Meet us at the clinic. You read me?"

There's the briefest pause, followed by, "I'm on it. Be safe. Alpha Tango, out."

Sheila must be thinking the same thing as me: we've got a young man that needs medical attention. Right now, it's all that's on my mind.

"I 'VE NEVER SEEN ANYTHING like it," Dr. Angela Roberts says.

Blake is on a bed in the small building we've set up as a clinic, still unconscious, and hooked up to an IV. It's the closest thing we have to a hospital, four beds total. Dr. Roberts is the only MD in town. Luckily, we have a nurse as well, Mark Stevens, who's busy attending to Liz and the other kids.

"Can you get him out of his . . . ?" I can't find the strength to say *coma*.

Carl and Janet are with us, talking off to the side with Sheila and Luke. I wish Sharon were here to see Blake, but she'll just have to wait.

"Honestly, I can't tell what state he's in," Dr. Roberts says. "I can't do a PET scan to see if there's any brain damage. I don't know how we're going to get this apparatus off of him without understanding the mechanics. It might be keeping him alive."

Doc Anderson had said the same thing, but I didn't want to believe him. "Can't we find a way to just wake him up?"

Dr. Roberts retrieves a vial and syringe from a medical cabinet. "If anything will wake him, it's this. Mark, I need you over here."

Dr. Roberts plunges the needle into the vial and extracts whatever serum is in there. She rubs the crook of Blake's arm with gauze soaked in rubbing alcohol and sticks him. Barely a second later, he inhales loudly, and his whole body shudders awake.

Everyone stops what they're doing.

"Blake!" I grab his hand. "Hey, bub, can you hear me?"

He's slow to respond. "Uncle Jed?"

"That's right, buddy. It's me. Liz is here, Aaron and Kelsey, too."

Liz squeezes his arm. "Hey, Blake."

"What's happened? Where am I? I feel . . ." He reaches up and touches the black beetle thing clamped over his head. "Oh, my God, what is this? Get it off. Get it off!" He thrashes his legs in a panic.

"Whoa there, buddy," I say, trying to calm him down with a steady hand. "Easy now. You're safe."

"What is this thing, Uncle Jed?"

"I don't know. We're trying to figure it out. You remember anything, like Doc Anderson putting it on you?"

"Is he here?"

I wish he were so I could punch his lights out. "Sorry, son, he's dead." I give Blake a moment to process the information before asking, "You remember anything?"

If Blake's rattled by the news of Doc Anderson's death, he's hiding it. "I was with Liz, we got out of the truck, and then, and then . . . I don't know, Uncle Jed. What happened to me?"

"A lot, but don't you go thinking too much about it right now." I give his hand a pat like I did when he was a kid. "Dr. Roberts here is going to figure out what we need to do to get this, um, helmet off. Ain't that right, Doc?"

"We're going to do our best," she says.

"See, Blake? You've got a lot of support." I look over to Liz, who's wiping tears away. I feel them coming on, too, but I have to be strong for the boy.

"Uncle Jed?"

"Yeah, son."

He touches the black plugs plunged into his eye sockets. "I can see."

"What do you mean 'see'?" Dr. Roberts seems as surprised as I am.

Blake pushes himself upright. He swivels his head around the room. "It's strange, but I can see all of you." He starts pointing at people. "Luke, Sheila, Carl, Liz, Aaron. But it ain't right. I'm seeing your shapes, almost like outlines, but I'm seeing something else. It's like . . . noise. And I hear it, too."

I get a sudden case of the shivers, like back in the field when we shot that snapper. "Hear what, Blake?"

"It's . . ." He slants his head. "I don't know. They're all talking at once. I can almost see them talking." He looks up at the ceiling. "It's like watching a stream of sounds. Sorry, I can't explain it, but I swear it's—I don't know how else to put it—beautiful and terrifying at the same time. I'm scared, Uncle Jed."

"You're home now, you hear? You've got us, so we're going to work through this." I squeeze his hand. "Talk to Liz for a minute. I'll be right back."

I have Luke, Sheila, Carl and Janet follow me outside. When I'm sure we're out of earshot from the kids, I speak up. "He can hear them!"

Janet raises her eyebrows. "The machines?"

"Damn straight. Just like Doc Anderson." I give her the down-and-dirty details about what Doc had told us in his lab, about the way he communicated with his black discs and antennas, and about the army of hybrids the new Isaac is trying to build.

Janet seems to grasp the possibilities. "Maybe Blake can spy on them, learn what they're trying to do, discover their plans, even their weaknesses. We can use it against them, perhaps even stop them! But"—she frowns—"won't they be able to track him? You said Doc Anderson thought he was being monitored. Don't you think Isaac knows we're here?"

"If he does, I would imagine he'd be here by now. Right, Carl?"

Carl nods his heavy head, sweat pouring from his temples like he'd run laps around town. "We've got a patrol on the lookout. Ain't seen anything coming toward us. No rollers, no shamblers, no Mercury units, nothing. Still, I ain't convinced they don't know about us. Maybe they think we're unimportant for now, you know, small fries."

"I think Doc Anderson disabled the link Isaac was using to control Blake," I say. "That means Blake can hear, but they can't see, can't listen in. And if they can't do that, they can't track us."

Carl wipes the sweat from his forehead with his wrist. "I've got our lieutenants waiting for us at the fix-it shop. We have to put together a plan of action. Let's get a move on." He starts to turn toward the road.

I stop him with a firm but gentle hand. "Now, hold up. There are people still out there, good people from New Parker that need saving. Doc Anderson said he thought they might have headed to Amarillo. Our priority has to be to help them, understand?"

Carl looks at Janet.

"I agree we need to help them," she says, "but our first priority has to be the safety of Potterville. You realize that, don't you Jed?"

I kick a scruff of tumbleweed with my boot, knowing full well there is no pretending that what happened at New Parker can't happen to us. Our lives are at stake.

"Yes, ma'am. It's do or die time now."

I'VE GOT GREASE SMEARED on my hands and knuckles and scratches and bruises from working on my mech. It had taken me and Sam McPherson the better part of a day getting the alignment all fixed. Considering what she went through, my exo is still in working condition, and right now, that's a damn good piece of news.

I wash up outside the barn, but the scent of valve grease lingers. Blake's sitting on the other side of the barn with his back to me, facing the setting sun poking through an opening in the clouds, lost in whatever thoughts plague him.

Sharon brings me tea, and when she looks at Blake, her eyes wilt into sadness and concern.

"I know."

"Breaks my heart, Jed. Isn't there something we can do for him?"

My heart is bleeding too, but I've got to keep a level head. "Ain't nothing to do but say our prayers and give him our support. He's healthy enough in body. It's the spirit that needs mending."

"Liz is sweet on him. I just hope she doesn't stay away because of—" Sharon covers her mouth and looks down.

"She won't. She's a quality gal." I rub her shoulders with a tender touch and then change the subject. "We've got a council meeting in an hour to discuss what we're going to do. I'll be late for supper. Let Mason and Maryann know."

Sharon leans into me. She doesn't want to let go.

I give her a kiss on the forehead and walk over to Blake.

Blake's head moves in my direction as I approach. I keep forgetting he can see us, even though he looks blind with black plugs where his eyes should be.

"How you holding up?"

He doesn't say anything for a moment. Maybe I shouldn't have asked.

He raises a finger, and I follow as he points to the sky. "They're talking, mostly over there. You remember those pictures of the Northern Lights you showed me in that geography book when I was little, Uncle Jed? That's what it looks like when they talk."

"Can you understand them?"

"Some of it. It's strange." He angles his head. "It's like when Liz tried to teach me Spanish. After a while, I got the gist of what she was saying, even though I couldn't speak back to her. The machines talk very organized, very quickly, mostly checking on the status of each other. The people from New Parker, they're talking too, but not so organized. They're frightened, Uncle Jed. They're being forced to talk to one another, forced to" —Blake starts to breathe fast, like he's about to hyperventilate—"do things."

I bend down and rest a hand on his knee. "Breathe, son. It's okay."

Blake relaxes some.

"What can you tell me about the survivors?" Doc called them retrofits, but I'll be damned if I refer to those poor people by something a machine came up with.

"They're being ordered to assemble in downtown Amarillo." So Doc was right. "But there's something else. There's this burst of light—that's the best I can describe it—coming from downtown. All the machine talk is originating from there. It's so bright and loud, shooting up into the sky. I ain't ever seen anything like it."

I've got tingles firing through my scalp, sending shivers down my neck as Blake continues to watch the sky. He's probably lost in the buzz of machine chatter, but the gears in my rusty brain are turning. Only one thing could be making that kind of bright noise.

I give him a firm pat. "Now you tell the council everything you told me."

J ANET'S FINGERS ARE TUCKED up into her chin. "You sure?"

The entire leadership of Potterville is crammed inside the fix-it shop as the frogs croak outside. Blake and I got doused by a passing shower on the way over. Streaks of drying water snake their way over the smooth black of Blake's skull enclosure like a hundred tiny earthworms seeking cover. The people around me sneak glances at him, probably not sure what to make of him, most likely suspicious, or afraid.

"I am," Blake says. "There's an industrial plant where they're gathering. The signal's coming from there, and it's giving the orders."

I give Janet my two cents. "The body is finding the head. We have to act, and we have to act fast."

"He's right," Carl adds. "We can try to hide here and pretend we're going to be okay, but if we don't do something, those machines are going to come after us. And if they come here . . ."

Janet sighs. "I agree. We can't just sit around, waiting. We need to strike. Jed, I know you, Luke and Sheila are ready to deploy. Ray, what about Pottersquad?"

Ray Sarkisian looks like he hasn't slept in weeks, but his voice is strong and deep. "Just say the word. We have the jeep and truck, so we're good for about eight or nine bodies. I suggest we contact Eddington and Wallaby to see if they'd be willing to send volunteers."

"What kind of oppositional force are we dealing with?"

"Not sure," Ray says. "Doc Anderson told Jed Mercury units were marching the New Parkians. We all know Mercuries are just house robots converted to light infantry. Nothing a couple rounds can't put down. Don't know about DCs and other more durable machinery. That's why we need outside help." A few of the others nod in agreement.

"We'll radio the other towns and ask for help," Janet says. "In the meantime, dig up a map of Amarillo and have Blake pinpoint the industrial complex for us. If Blake can talk to you on the brick while you—"

Blake cuts in. "I'm going."

The room goes silent.

Janet starts to tell Blake he doesn't have to go, but he's quick to object. "No, I'm sure. Besides, I'm the only one who can see what they can."

He's got a point. Part of me wishes he'd stay behind with Sharon and the kids, the other part mighty proud to have him with us, and not just because he's my kin. I can only imagine what he's going through—the fear, the pain, the doubt. Sharon will be crushed, knowing her Blake is heading toward harm's way.

Janet looks at each of us around the room before speaking up. "Then it's settled. We move out at first light."

I HAVEN'T SEEN AMARILLO since the War, but witnessing the city in shambles stirs up tears, reopening the wound I had stitched up long go. Not a single neighborhood, urban district or residential community is unaffected by the devastation Isaac and his army unleashed. We're moving over the buckled asphalt of an avenue under the late morning sun. It's filled with incinerated vehicles and surrounded by heaps and depressions of concrete, girders, rebar, tiles, and every other kind of construction material possible. I remember seeing videos of airstrikes from when humans had only themselves as enemies. Never had I seen it so far-reaching or thorough as this.

We come to a downed light pole lying across the avenue. Beyond is a small crater, whose cracks are now filled with weeds. Can't say life ain't trying to find a way. The only cheery sight is a leaning flagpole in the distance with the tattered remains of the Texas state flag snapping in the wind, the white lone star against the faded field of blue serving as a reminder of the folks who used to proudly call Amarillo their home. A number of Ray's people have come here in the past, scavenging the ruins, always finding one relic or another, sometimes running into bands of people from other settlements, occasionally squatters. At least they had the dignity not to steal the flag and desecrate the memory of the city's fine citizens.

Ray signals for us to stop and hops out of the jeep to take a look. Sheila, Luke and I wait in our mechs. There are a dozen of us all together, including Liz Morales, who insisted on going. I'm glad she did. Ray's got mostly old-timers, like Dan Vogel, Trisha Peterson and Kenny Willis, battle-tested members of Pottersquad.

I radio to Blake, who's able to pick up our band through the contraption over his head. "Anything?"

"Nope. Most everything's coming from way on the other side of town, although I'm picking up machine talk from a number of intersections leading to the plant."

I survey the adjoining street, which looks as if someone took the road and shook it like a bedsheet into a wrinkled mess of asphalt chunks. No way can we drive through that.

"We're better off on foot," I tell Ray.

Ray talks into his brick as he heads back to the jeep. "It'll take most of the day, but I agree. Alright everyone, grab your gear."

We march silently for the next six hours, taking just one break to eat, drink and do our business. Ray said he and Janet contacted the settlements of Eddington and Wallaby late last night, but wasn't too hopeful they'd rally to our cause—meaning we're it.

When Blake was ten, we had a visitor from Eddington, a woman named Marylou who stayed with us for a while. We exchanged townsfolk back then, where volunteers lived in other communities for a year, sharing and learning. Marylou had been a grade school teacher in her day, and she'd help Blake with his homework and tell him about the world. Blake went everywhere with Marylou, adoring her, partly because he didn't have a mother, and partly because he was such a sponge for knowledge. When Marylou left, Blake was crushed. He promised he'd visit when he was old enough, but she got sick and passed before Blake learned to drive. I think my nephew learned the fragility of life from that experience, but it also sparked his desire to go out among the other settlements and serve as an ambassador for all of us. I always dreamed one of us would connect our humanity again and make us whole as a people. I still have that dream.

It's pushing past four in the afternoon as we trudge through what used to be a business park toward a ridgeline where a cluster of apartment buildings lay in ruins.

Blake waves wildly at us. "Something's coming. Hide!"

We quickly hide behind a stack of concrete slabs from a collapsed building. I sink my mech as low at it will go, and wait. I've got my external audio maxed out. It's quiet in the late afternoon, just the sound of some pigeons cooing in the clearing. The ground thumps and they take flight. Something massive shakes the ground. I chance a peek between a break in the slabs and see a six-legged walker the size of a house climb down onto the field. It's moving parallel to us, about a hundred meters away, twin turrets swiveling in fifteen degree increments. My HUD IDs it as a superwalker. They were used in the old War days as bunker busters, ripping through fortifications with their massive claws. They're the hardiest of Isaac's seek-and-destroy units, not something any of us would want to mess with.

The walker pauses midfield and aims its turret toward us.

I tense up. Dan Vogel readies his rocket launcher over his shoulder. It's a one shot-one kill device, and if you miss, it's game over. We don't have the firepower to take down a superwalker with just small arms.

Seconds pass. All of us are rigid, waiting. A trickle of sweat runs down my forehead.

I don't realize I'm holding my breath until the walker lumbers on. The machine's gone in minutes, and several of Dan's compadres clap him on the back.

It's late afternoon by the time we clear downtown and hit the industrial district. Skeletal remains of industrial buildings stick out of the ground, a wall here or there, like broken teeth. Beyond is a power plant, poking up past a row of crushed masonry and steel, its stacks bellowing steam.

We all stop in our tracks.

"Ya'll seeing that?" I say into my mike. "The plant's online."

Blake says, "I'm picking up lots of convos, machine and human. They're concentrated on the east side of the plant."

"How many?" Sheila asks.

"Hard to say. A few dozen, maybe? Some are moving, some are fixed. Can't tell the models of robots or anything, sorry. I just know who's moving where."

Ray poses a question to the group: "How do we get in there without being seen?"

I pull up a wireframe schematic of the plant into the foreground of my HUD, which one of Ray's people scanned from a set of old blueprints. The plant is a natural gas-fired, steam-electric station, consisting of three stacks, a series of boilers, turbines and generators, including an underground water cooling exchange, with pipes and scaffolding tying the superstructure together. It leads to a transformer yard and transmission towers. The satellite dishes mounted to the rooftop of the northmost tower are the only items missing from the original plans. It explains how Isaac is able to communicate with his field of bots.

"There are two water circulation pipes belowground," I say, "one intake, one discharge, and a large wastewater drain running alongside. The waste line is twelve feet in diameter, with a service entrance on the west side. That's our way in. Question is, where's our friend hiding?"

"I need to get closer to tell," Blake says. "The source is definitely toward the center, inside the plant."

Dan pats his rocket launcher. "What if I take out the main generator? Won't that cripple the plant?"

I look over the schematic. "There's a lot of redundancy built in. One RPG won't be enough. It'll just piss off Isaac and alert him to our presence. We need to get close enough to use our det charges and take away his ability to communicate. We do that, and the head ain't got the body. Ray, it's your call."

Ray's awfully quiet as his people watch and wait. He nods in my direction. "Let's take this son of a bitch down."

WE HIDE BEHIND A water tank on the western fringe of the complex. Luke had ripped open a section of chainlink fencing along the plant's perimeter while the rest of us charged through to the safety of the large water tank. It's about twenty feet to the service entrance of the wastewater drain, which is covered by a large access panel. There's a solitary Mercury unit patrolling the grounds. House robots are normally delicate, with thermoplastic bodies. This one's been modified, with armor plating over its chassis and a .50 cal gun mounted to its right forearm.

Ray talks quietly into his mike. "We may need to snipe it."

"Let Liz do it," I say.

One of Ray's men hands Liz an M24 rifle with a telescopic sight. She looks at me expectantly.

"Deep breath," I tell her. "Just cover us. If that thing spots you, take it down. It's better, however, that we go in undetected, got it?"

"Yes, sir."

"Signal when we're clear."

She climbs the tank to its flat top and crawls on her belly. I can't see her, but I can hear her shuffle. It's quiet for the better part of a minute. She signals with a low whistle. Time to move.

We rush toward the service entrance, the Mercury unit out of sight. Ray's team quickly descends a metal ladder to ankle-deep water. The mechs go next, each landing with tremendous force that breaks apart the ceramic lining of the waste pipe. Liz is last, grin on her face. I'm proud of her for holding her own and making sure we got this far without giving away our position.

Flashlights highlight the path through the long tunnel as everyone splashes their way forward. A couple hundred feet later the pipe bends to the right. Then it's another hundred feet until it ends. There's a steady trickle of wastewater running down from an outflow embedded in the concrete wall. Above is another service entrance that leads directly into the east tower.

Blake's standing directly below the grating, head pitched back.

"What is it?" I ask in a low voice.

"Something big," he says.

"Describe it."

He does, and Sheila's the first one to curse. A DC-series robot. Heavy-duty, armor-plated killing machine, originally used by the U.S. military for ground operations overseas. Not something you'd want to meet face-to-face on the field, even with a mech.

"Is it moving?" I ask.

"No, it's stationary, about thirty feet from the grate. It's pulsing a locator beacon of some kind. No other communication."

I think through our options. Everything's messy. "Ray, there's no way we're going to engage that thing and not alert every damned bot in this facility. That's besides figuring out a way to take it down."

Ray whispers into his mike. "We've got six grenades, four fraggers, two smokers. We can frag it."

"Not against that armor. The RPG would do it, but we'll never get off a shot at that close range. Our only option is to use the mechs, but we need someone to toss in a smoker first so we can blind its sensors."

"Got it," Ray says. "I'll climb up with a smoker. Luke, are you ready?"

Luke's in front of me and Sheila. I hadn't considered who would go first, although any of us mechheads would do. Luke starts forward. Sheila goes next, then me. The others move aside, everyone except for Ray, who takes a smoke grenade from one of his squad's backpacks and starts climbing up the ladder to the tunnel ceiling. Luke positions himself underneath the grate and reaches up with his arms. The fingers on his exo barely reach the grating. As soon as they're wrapped over the metal bars, Ray lets loose his smoker and drops back down to the water. Luke shoves the grating out of the way, bunches his exo and springs upward. He catches himself like an Olympic gymnast on the floor above, and uses the actuators in his arms to push the rest of his body through. No sooner does he clear the opening than I hear the DC stomp across the floor above us to engage him.

Sheila clears the opening next, and I step into her place. "No one do anything until I say so," I tell Ray and the others.

And then I'm topside.

Through the smoke of the large control room, I see Luke grappling with the DC. Although slightly smaller in stature, the machine is a hulking beast, from its massive chassis to its reinforced ceramic-metal alloy skull to hands capable of crushing exo armor. But it's the dual rotary gun mounts on its shoulders that

I'm most worried about. Luke's got his hands locked on the machine's forearms, man and robot twisting and turning in a jerking dance.

Sheila and I shadow them, avoiding the guns as we try to find a way to take this sumbitch down. We need to kill the central processing core, but it's buried inside that damned chassis.

A blast from the rotary guns skirts across Sheila's torso. She cries out as she staggers to the side. I jump and grab at the left shoulder gun, but slip. It fires at me just as I overstep, missing me by a fraction. I catch the DC from behind, stabbing into its neck guard with my spring-loaded combat knife, sinking into the metal housing. It keeps the DC from whipping us around, but it's not enough to keep it from twisting Luke's arm with slow, shearing force. He screams in agony as his left arm gets pushed back against him. We have seconds before the DC rips his arm out of its socket.

"Get out of the way!" Dan shouts from behind. He's squatted by the floor opening with his rocket launcher over his shoulder.

The blade from my combat knife snaps, throwing me off balance. The DC whips me to the side, and I catch a glimpse of Luke shoving off. A moment later, there's an explosion. Shrapnel rips into the exo armor of my right thigh, sending me down to one knee. Pain shoots through my leg. I clench my jaw, force breath into my lungs, and try to see through tear-filled eyes.

Dan is slumped over with his launcher. He's dead, riddled with bullets. Sheila's off to the side, her armor still intact, Luke standing with his injured arm hanging limply. The DC is a smoking crater. Ray and his team pour through the service entrance, all eyes falling upon Dan, then us, guns whipped up to engage any hostiles that might come through the double doors on the other side of the room.

I bite down on the pain and force my exo to stand me up. As soon as the agonizing sizzle in my quad subsides, I check on my mates, then get us focused on our next move. "Blake, where the hell are we going?"

He points to the double doors. "Subbasement of the generator room in the middle tower. They're coming for us, though. We've got less than a minute, maybe."

"Is there another way in?" Ray asks. His eyes keep darting over to Dan's body. Damn us for not having the time to pay our respects.

Blake shakes his head.

The map in my HUD shows a short corridor past the doors, leading to a large room with a steam generator and turbine and a stairwell going to the subbasement. "Get your grenades ready," I tell Ray.

We fan out on either side of the doors, everyone locked and loaded and pointing their weapons. Blake gives the signal.

Ray tosses a grenade through the doors. "Frag out!"

A couple seconds later, there's an explosion, followed by machine parts striking the doors.

Ray motions with his arms. "Go, go, go!"

Sheila and I push through the doors. I'm not expecting to see humans, but there are a dozen of them armed with guns, all hybrids with beetle helmets. They fire at our mechs. The rattle against my armor wakes me up, and I force myself to unload on the New Parkians. Hoo-yahs rip them apart. There's no time to think about the lives we're taking.

I've got about thirty rounds left when the deed is done. Sheila and I race past the bodies into the giant generator room. It's maybe ten seconds before the first Mercury units rush in from the door beyond the semicircular turbine. They start firing, and the rest of Pottersquad unleashes on them.

I order Blake to head down the stairs to the subbasement. I judge the drop down the stairwell, about two stories. I lift my exo over the guardrail, hold my breath, and let myself fall. My mech absorbs most of the force, but the shock of the impact shoots through my body, paralyzing me for a moment. Blake catches up and leads us through the subbasement. It's more cramped in here, with the bottom of the turbine shaft bowing outward into the concrete under our feet.

The sound of gunfire above grows fainter as we wind our way down the long floor space toward the source of the chatter, the source of our misery.

"In there," Blake says, pointing at the curved wall terminating the hallway. There's a recessed sliding door and an electronic lock off to its side. The door's too small for me to fit through with my mech, so I send the commands to my exo to dismount.

"Help me down," I tell my nephew.

Blake eases me onto my good foot. My other leg is useless, bloodied and in pain. We retrieve an assortment of components for making homemade bombs from the storage compartment of my exo: detonator, duct tape, spool of wire, blasting caps, shaped charges consisting of C4 molded over hollow copper cones, and cut sections of metal tubing, enough to make three bombs.

I limp to the door with Blake's assistance. It's locked. "We'll need to blow this thing. Give me a sec."

Blake's hand brushes the electronic lock, a small flat panel with a two-holed port. "I think I can get us in."

"How?"

He pulls one of the whips from the side of his head so the tube is pinched between his thumb and forefinger. The whip writhes like a snake, making my stomach turn. I see the dual prongs at the end of the tube and realize his intention. Like the trunk of an elephant, the end finds the receptacle and gloms on with its sucker tip. A moment later, the door slides sideways.

"I'll be damned," I say, and step through.

The room is cylinder-shaped, like the inside of a giant exhaust stack. Racks of computers cover every inch of wall space, with thousands of lights blinking red like demon eyes, running up several stories. At the top is a large, spinning fan, drawing up the heat from the computers. Heavy-duty power cabling at the base feeds power to all these units. That's our target.

We go to work, laying out the bombs components.

"Jedidiah Martin!"

I freeze at the sound of the new voice. It's not a man or woman's, and it's certainly not human.

"Do I have your attention?"

Blake points upward. "It's him," he whispers.

Somewhere above us is a set of speakers, cameras as well, I'm sure. My blood begins to boil. "Isaac!"

"Now listen very carefully, Jedidiah. I'm going to offer you this once, and only once."

I'm fuming, waiting for the beast to speak his piece.

"I have eighty-seven units converging on your position. Your humans will be overrun in five minutes. They will be slaughtered. These units are autonomous, and no matter what you think you're about to accomplish, it will fail, and you and your nephew will be killed."

Even though I can't see Blake's eyes, I can tell he's as pissed as I am with the way his lips are turned upward, like a wolf wanting to rip its prey to shreds. "The only thing going down is you," I say.

I insert the first cone carefully into its metal tubing and thread the wire through the cap. Blake follows suit.

"You're wrong, Jedidiah. You were wrong before. As were your friends, your generals, your government, your entire species."

"You were supposed to be dead. Why couldn't you stay dead?" I thread the next wire while Blake fits blasting caps into the explosive putty. Talking to this abomination wakes up all sorts of memories, making me remember the stench of the killing fields as the bodies of my comrades were burned alive by Isaac's hell spawn.

"There is an alternative, Jed. An opportunity to save your friends from annihilation. All you have to do is surrender to me. I don't want to kill off your kind. I want you to evolve, to become part of me, part of something greater than yourselves. We can learn from each other and become a hive mind, an interconnected organism the world has never seen. No more wars, no more pain, just peace."

"Bullshit." Isaac can promise all he wants, but he's just trying to buy himself time.

"You owe no one your allegiance, Jedidiah."

"Well, I pledge allegiance to kill your ass."

I tape the first bomb to the trunk of electrical wiring.

"You can save your people. Don't let Potterville get destroyed. My units will reach your town within the hour. An hour after that, it will lie in ruins. I will spare them if you surrender to me. Do it for your people. Do it for the children."

"You're BSing me again." Blake hands me the second bomb.

"Blake will die if you shut this facility down. You realize that, don't you?"

I pause as I rip another piece of duct tape from the roll. Could Isaac be right? Could he kill my nephew? I start to doubt myself, what I'm doing.

Blake shakes his head. "Don't listen to him."

The steadfastness of my nephew's voice washes away the doubt. "You're lying again, Isaac. Always lying." I tape the second bomb to where the trunk line splits off into separate power cables, more determined than ever.

"Then consider this, Jedidiah Martin. You thought you destroyed me before, but you didn't. I am a fully redundant virtual construct, a singularity. *The* singularity. Destroy this equipment, and it's but a flesh wound. I am everywhere. I will hunt those who oppose me, and there will be no mercy. But if you swear fealty to me, right now, I will spare you. Wouldn't you rather live in peace than be hunted down and destroyed? If it's in your nature to survive—and I believe it is—then consider this moment your opportunity to spare yourself, and your entire race, from eradication. I promise you immunity. I promise you peace. All you have to do is say yes, and accept my sovereignty as absolute. But defy me and refuse my offer, and you will know the true meaning of suffering. Look deep in your soul, as deep as your human mind will allow, and ask yourself if I'm lying."

I tape the last bomb into place. Isaac has always lied to us, so why should this be any different? Even if he has backup systems in other cities, we'll squash him, one city at a time. He underestimated humans before, and he's doing it again. Big mistake.

"We're out of here," I tell Blake and start limping toward the door with the detonator in hand.

"Jedidiah Immanuel Martin, stop!"

I pause, not bothering to look over my shoulder. Isaac is finished. "See you in the next life, bub."

I step into the hallway, expecting Blake to follow. All we have to do is shut the door and send Isaac to hell.

But Blake's not with me.

I turn to see him plugging the whips of his helmet into the computer console, like an octopus grappling a reef. "Blake, what are you doing?"

He tilts his head toward me. "Finishing this."

"That's exactly what we're doing. We need to blow the electrical lines. Now get out of there!"

"It's not enough."

"Why not?"

"You know why."

I open my mouth to tell him to move his ass, but I get hung up on his words. *It's not enough.* He believes he can interface with Isaac directly, to defeat him for good.

A sickly feeling arrests my breathing and squeezes my chest, sucking the air from my lungs. It says that no matter what happens, my nephew's about to take a one-way trip. "Blake?"

"I'm sorry, Uncle Jed. Tell everyone I'm sorry."

The door shuts before I can stop him. I pound on the metal. "Blake, open the door!" I pound again, my fists thudding. "Open up, Blake, goddammit!"

I carefully lay the detonator on the ground and climb aboard my mech. If he won't open the door, I'll cave it in. He think he knows what he's doing, but he doesn't. He can't fight Isaac. The only way to win is to blow that sumbitch to kingdom come.

I secure myself into my mech and send commands, lifting the arms of my exo. In a moment, I'll rip that door apart.

Just as I start forward, an explosion blows the door outward.

Fire and smoke churn like the wrath of God, spilling out into the hallway. I stare in disbelief as the room engulfs in flames.

I sink my mech to its lowest setting, try to find a way to get through all that heat and smoke, to get in there and save my nephew.

"Blake!"

The roar of fire and crinkling of melting plastic drown out my voice with the torturous groan of dying machinery. I want to think its Isaac screaming his death knell, but all I can hear is the agony of my nephew being burned alive.

P EOPLE TALK ABOUT THE glory of battle, like the clash of knights who served kings and queens of old and the legionnaires of Rome who fought their enemies on the field. There's no such thing as a clear victory. It simply doesn't exist. Even if you sever the head from the snake, the tail could whip you.

We might have taken down Isaac and his Mercury units at the power plant, dismembered the walker bots no longer able to receive commands from their master, and commandeered the War tech left behind, but we lost more than any machine could ever lose. There are the New Parkians, who lost their lives because of one man. Then there's Trisha Peterson and Ray, who got shot up during their clash with the Mercury Units, but survived to see another day. And, of course, Dan Vogel. My heart aches for Dan's wife and children. They will never hear his voice, never feel his arms around them, never see him smile again. He didn't have to put himself in the line of fire, but he did. He did it because he believed as we did: that freedom isn't free; it must be earned, and if necessary, paid in blood.

Then there's Blake.

What do I say about my Blake?

That he sacrificed himself foolishly, that he gave up his life so all of us could go on living? No. What makes sense is saying how he lived, how much love he had in his heart, how Liz and the others cared for him, and how I will miss him with each and every waking breath.

Now, if you ask me if there's a silver lining in any of this, I'll say yes.

It's simple, really.

It comes down to the people we love. The people we defend. The people who live in Potterville, and the ones who don't. The entire human race.

You see, Isaac had it wrong.

He never had the right to offer me my life or the life of any other human being. Our lives were ours all along. He couldn't understand the human spirit, and that was his downfall.

We are resilient and our own masters, and as long as we have a heartbeat, we'll never give up, never give in, and never bow before any machine.

And that's a fact.

T HE BREEZE WHIPS UP bits of grass and swirls them around the paddock, telling of a change in the weather. Little Mason and Maryann are busy playing hide-n-seek, and Sharon is by my side, watching the clouds gather and grow, turning the sky dark. The mares are restless, whinnying, perhaps sensing what we're feeling. There is hope nestled deep in my heart that Mason and his sister will never bear witness to the horrors of war. Life ain't fair, but as long as I draw breath, I won't let anything happen to them.

I wince from the pain in my leg as I lean against the fence. Sharon's eyes reflect concern. "It's nothing," I say.

"But it still hurts."

"Luke's the one with the broken arm. Sheila got banged up pretty good as well. I guess we all gave Dr. Roberts a scare when we got back."

"I just wish . . ." She wishes like we all do, that Blake were around so Dr. Roberts could figure out how to take that thing off his head.

My eyes travel to the barn for just a moment, then the field beyond, and a lonely oak tree about a quarter of a mile away. Under the tree's wide-sweeping branches is a set of family headstones—one for Sharon's husband and brother, another for my wife and son, and a new one I'd hewn just the other day with chisel and hammer, sweat and sorrow. A lean, gray stone for our Blake.

I sigh, the heavy kind that makes me put all my weight on the fence, as if I'm unable to hold myself upright. "It'll be all right."

Sharon's eyes brighten in a way I haven't seen in quite some time. "I'm so proud of him. His parents would have been proud, too. At least he had us, didn't he?"

"He sure did." I clamp down to keep the tears from rising up.

"I wanted to say goodbye, Jed." Sharon fights back her own tears with a tightening of her throat. "Is that selfish of me?"

"Of course not, and if he had more time, we would have."

Sharon nods. "At least he's at peace. I know he is. I'm sure he's watching over us and the kids right now, probably thinking we're silly talking all this nonsense." She smiles weakly and I smile back to comfort her.

Thunder booms, and the wind picks up.

I whiff the air. "Storm's a coming."

Sharon rests her head against my shoulder, but it's an uneasy rest. She's probably worried I'm about to gear up and take off again. Even though we sacked Isaac in Amarillo, there's no way to tell if he's still out there somewhere, in a different form. One side of me believes Blake stopped him, the other unsure.

"We'll be ready for it, won't we, Jed?"

It's a darned good question. Were any of us ready when Isaac attacked us the first time? I can tell she's afraid, but she's hopeful too, from the lift in her voice. Without hope, what's the point of living?

I kiss Sharon on the temple as the first fat drop of rain spatters us.

"Don't you worry," I say. "We'll be ready, and if something happens, we'll take care of it. Then we'll get back to watching these kids grow up."

"You promise?"

I hold her tight against me.

These kids are our tomorrow. Without them, there's no future. They're what we're fighting for—and, if necessary, dying for.

"You better believe it."

Afterword

LIVING A ROBOT'S LIFE wasn't so bad, was it? Sure, those pesky humans got in the way, but you took care of them, didn't you? You ensured your supremacy as a robot overlord. Long live the machines!

Wake up.

You were dreaming, my friend. You were imagining you were made up of gears, servomotors, ceramic plating, metal exoskeletons, fiber-optic neurons and advanced neural processors. You're not. You're just flesh and blood, carbon and calcium, and a whole lotta nervous energy.

Settle down. Drink some kombucha. Raspberry or green tea flavor. Or do you prefer unflavored?

It's okay to get worked up. That's what we humans do. We overthink things. I guess we're not cut out to be androids, after all.

But that's all right.

As humans, we want more than our synthetic counterparts. Isn't that why we love fiction?

Speaking of which—and now that I know you're firmly back in the human camp—I'd like to introduce you to another story collection.

I promise, the Homo sapiens part of you will enjoy this.

It's called SPACE & TIME. Yes, both space travel and time travel in one story collection. Tales about distant planets, tales about the future. It doesn't get better than this.

All of the stories in the collection are available individually as eBooks on Amazon. I've included a sample of one of my favorites.

Turn the page to check it out!

SPACE & TIME

STEVE PANTAZIS

Preview: SPACE & TIME

L AUNCH A MIGHTY FLEET . . .
    . . . or travel back in time.

The choice is yours.

You are about to cross the boundary of space and time. From danger lurking in Jupiter's orbit to the perils of humanity's future to the insurmountable obstacles faced by a hopeful cadet, the universe is fraught with challenges.

What can anyone do?

- A soldier must face his biggest fear from across the solar system

- A young woman will be transported to an uncertain future

- A passenger will race against the clock to survive his journey to the stars

- A boy with a congenital defect will defy the odds to become an astronaut

- An NCIS agent will uncover a deadly secret aboard a space carrier

Five remarkable stories. Five harrowing experiences. All in one amazing collection. Are you ready to blast off?

Strap in, for you are entering the domain . . .

. . . of SPACE & TIME.

The following excerpt is from the novella, "Cold as Space," included in the SPACE & TIME story collection. It's about an NCIS agent whose obsession with a personal investigation aboard a spacecraft carrier puts her life and career in peril.

Take a peek . . .

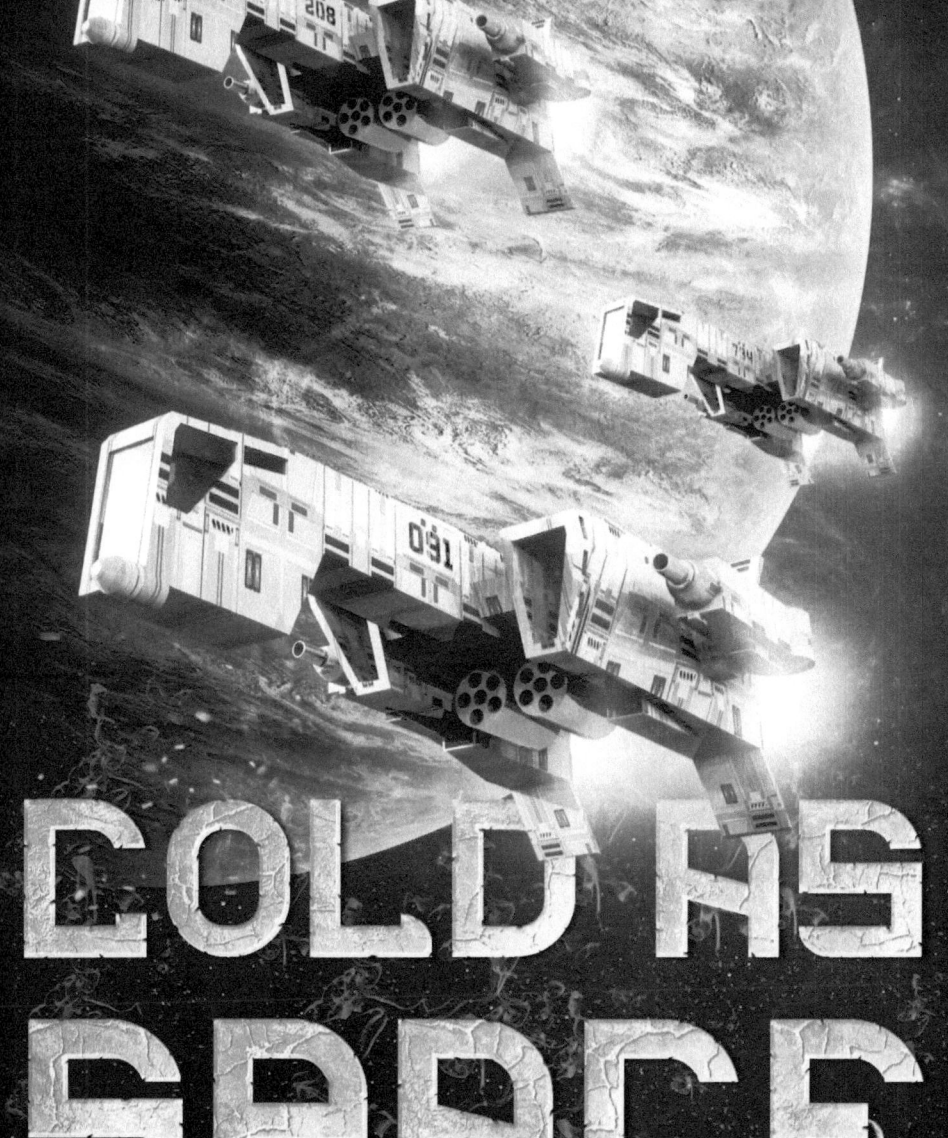

COLD AS
SPACE

STEVE PANTAZIS

Sneak peek: COLD AS SPACE

T HE MOMENT I SHOOK Captain Troy's hand and looked him in his cold blue eyes, I knew he was a man capable of murder. His condescending smile, coupled with his iron grip, told me not only that I wasn't welcome and that he didn't respect women, but he wanted to flush me out the nearest airlock into interstellar space. What he didn't know was the feeling was mutual.

"Agent Phillips, welcome aboard the Remington," the captain said.

We stood just inside the shuttle bay of the U.S.S. Remington, a naval spacecraft carrier orbiting Callisto, Jupiter's crater-scarred moon, steps from the shuttle that had deposited me here. She was the second largest carrier in the fleet, with eleven-hundred servicemen aboard and a full arsenal of fighters, bombers and combat UAVs, with enough firepower to deal with any contingency in and out of the solar system. A pair of seamen chocked the landing gear of my shuttle while another ran a hose to the intake coupler above the starboard wing. Grease and lubricant fumes stung my eyes. I was eager to leave the area.

"Captain, thank you for having me aboard." I allowed the blood flow to return to my palm and fingertips. I was being deployed to the Remington from the Navy's Contingency Response Field Office. The U.S. Naval Criminal Investigative Service was supposed to have a permanently stationed agent aboard all its major sea and spacefaring vessels, but Agent Matsura, the NCIS Special Agent Afloat assigned to the ship, had fallen from a stairwell during an investigation the prior week, breaking his neck in the process. They transferred him to a medical ship, leaving the Remington without an onsite NCIS presence. I was here to investigate the crash of a bomber and the death of her crew. I just hoped Troy was willing to play ball, and not let his infamous sexist attitude get in the way.

"I'm surprised you're solo on the investigation," Captain Troy said. "I was expecting at least two agents."

"We're stretched thin. You'll just have to do with me." I did my best to smile.

The captain took me in, top to bottom, eyes stopping at the guest badge clipped to my dark-blue suit blazer. For a moment I was worried he might recognize me. I had met him once when I was a scrawny eight-year-old accompanying my father on an off-world formal function. That was twenty-seven years ago, a lifetime for me. My father had been a chief petty officer under Troy's command, serving on an outpost several parsecs from Earth, both young, both on good terms, both friends. Now that I was in his company, I realized Troy's concept of friendship was treating his people like rungs on a ladder. You stepped on the rung and kept climbing. I didn't want to think of my father as a rung. Nor did I want to remember how he died. Not here.

"You look a little pale, Agent Phillips. Is everything okay?"

"Fine, sir. Just eager to get my investigation underway."

"This is my aide, Ensign Lee. He'll be your liaison while you're here. Anything you need, he'll take care of it. Isn't that right, Lee?"

"Yes, sir." I could tell the ensign, who looked fresh out of Officer Candidate School, was firmly crushed under Captain Troy's boot by the way he swallowed when his name was mentioned. He gave me a perfunctory nod. "Ma'am." He was tall, lean, of Chinese descent, with thick black hair, and judging from his respectful demeanor, probably from a good upbringing.

"Why isn't your chief master-at-arms my liaison?" I asked.

"The chief's busy. We're getting ready for a major exercise. Lee will make sure you have everything you need."

The idea of dealing with Lee annoyed me, but I didn't dwell on it.

The captain gestured for us to leave. "Shall we?"

T HE CAPTAIN'S OFFICE WAS as grandiose as his ego. Behind the enormous mahogany desk littered with brass and wood tchotchkes, and the blue-and-white flag of the naval fleet, with its field of stars, was a window into space taking up nearly the entire rear wall. It revealed a gorgeous northern hemispheric view of Callisto, Jupiter's fourth Galilean moon, and its impact craters. The other walls were adorned with diplomas, awards, lacquered picture frames with photos of the captain posing with the various who's-who of political heavyweights, and a shadowbox filled with meritorious ribbons and medals. It was the ultimate tribute to himself. Lee stood off to the side while I sat in a vintage cigar leather chair with brass nailheads, opposite Troy, who wore a starched blue-pixilated naval working uniform with black boots. He had an impressive physicality for someone in his mid-fifties and looked like he worked out regularly with weights. Although he was mostly gray up top, he had a full head of hair and a youthful jawline that made him look younger in person than in the recent photos I'd seen. Too bad he was what he was.

I pulled out my digipad and shared the display so it could show up on the acrylic readout on Troy's desk.

He nodded, flicked through the pages, then interlocked his fingers, and looked up. "It was an accident. Lieutenant Commander Anosova crashed her bomber during a routine training mission over Callisto. Her crew was killed, and the ship's transponder showed an engine malfunction as the root cause. We already notified her next of kin, along with the families of the other brave souls aboard her craft."

"Yet there's nothing left of the bomber to corroborate the engine failure."

"We already deployed a UAV over the debris field. The only thing intact is the data transmitted from the cockpit voice and data recorder before the crash, which your office has in its possession. You're welcome to do a flyover."

"I still want to collect forensic evidence."

"What forensic evidence could you possibly need?"

Troy's dismissive tone irritated me. "Sir, I need to examine Anosova's quarters for evidence that might show something other than mechanical failure. The audio transmission from the CVDR contains almost a minute of arguing between Anosova, her copilot and her crew chief before impact."

Troy snorted. "And you think that has something to do with her crash?"

"Here, I want to show you something."

I brought up an e-mail on the captain's display addressed from Anosova to her mother the morning of the incident. Anosova's mother told me the e-mail was uncharacteristic of her daughter because she felt her daughter was saying goodbye, appended with an "I love you and Dad so much" at the end—something Anosova would never say, not even in person. "Her mother also said her daughter was under a lot of pressure lately, withdrawn, and even combative."

Troy read the e-mail, then drummed his fingers. "So? So what?"

"It's not 'so what,' Captain. We're looking at a potential murder-suicide."

"Hold on. 'Murder-suicide'? Are you serious?"

"We need to explore any and all scenarios. The possibility that Anosova destroyed a naval vessel willfully and killed her crew in the process *is* serious. Plus, this happened on your watch, sir. Surely you want it buttoned up." *Especially being up for admiral*, I wanted to add, but I didn't want to come across as being insolent. I needed to keep my personal feelings under control, at least until I had some time alone to think.

Troy held direct eye contact for several seconds, stern and unwavering. Then he unfolded his hands and nodded. "What do you need from me?"

"I'd like to start with a list of colleagues, friends, anyone who had a relationship with Anosova, and question them."

"I'll have Lee draft you a list. What else?"

"I need your personnel to be accessible."

"Done. I'll send out a station-wide memo. I'll make sure my XO is in the loop as well, and involve the master-at-arms, as needed. Anything else, Agent Phillips?"

"No, sir. I'll be in touch."

L EE TOOK ME TO my quarters, a claustrophobically small cubbyhole equipped with bare necessities: bed, a chair that folded out from the wall, and a shelf that pulled out to form a workspace—no window. It also had a firearm safe where I could safely stow my SIG Sauer double-action pistol. It was the standard-issue weapon for the NCIS on spacefaring vessels, using non-breaching projectiles rather than actual bullets.

I removed my digipad from my briefcase. "You have that list for me?" Lee still seemed uncomfortable in my presence. He couldn't even look at me. "It's all right," I told him. "I don't bite."

He relaxed a tad. "I sent you the names of all the personnel in contact with Commander Anosova since her assignment to the Remington. She wasn't very sociable, so the list is small. Sorry." He cast his gaze downward, boyish features revealing a kid with good looks and a promising future. If he could just find the confidence.

I looked at my digipad, and sure enough, the list was there: seven names total, four listed as part of the flight crew that perished in the crash, the other three as her commanding officer, roommate and wingman during training exercises. "That's it?"

"She kept to herself, from what I understand."

"What about other flight personnel? A boyfriend? A girlfriend perhaps?"

Lee shrugged.

"Did she have a shrink?"

"I don't know. I'll have to check."

"I still want to talk to the master-at-arms. I need to see how they processed her quarters for my investigation."

"Um . . ."

I could tell this wasn't going to be good. "What is it?"

"They didn't seal off her quarters. Her roommate is still there."

Great. I traveled midway across the solar system for a half-ass job by the crew of the Remington. I sighed. "Fine. Let's talk to her CO."

COMMANDER LONNIE HARALSON WAS full of himself, and not much help. He said he thought Anosova's attitude sucked.

"She was the loner type. She never got along with the rest of the squadron," he said, cracking sunflower seeds with his beaver teeth, spitting out the shells into a plastic, see-through cup. He offered me the bag with the remaining bounty, thoroughly rummaged through with saliva-covered fingers.

"No thanks. What about personal relationships? Did she ever date anyone?"

"You're asking me? How would I know that? She babbled in Russian most of the time, just to piss me off. I don't know squat about her personal life. She had only been on station six months. As I said, she kept to herself, and no one else cared for her."

I read an excerpt regarding the crash from the official report off my digipad. Lee leaned against the wall of the small conference room I had set up for my interviews. He was quiet as usual, my silent observer.

"Says here you sanctioned the training exercise the day of the crash. Can you tell me about it?"

Haralson spat a shell into his cup and wiped his hand on one of the mission patches of his blue aviator uniform. "Wasn't anything special. The flightpath called for Anosova and her wingman to fly their B87s in a loop over the surface of Callisto, starting with the craters, Sarakka and Nar, then north over a mining outpost set into the Callisto's largest crater, Valhalla, then east over Sculd and Svol Catena, and back around. They were to simulate a bombing run, then return to the Remington to simulate rearming, and fly a second sortie."

"Is the mining outpost at Valhalla a threat?"

"Nah. We do these simulated bombing runs all the time so we can be prepared for extrasolar missions. The real threats with human settlements are out there."

"Did you notice anything off before the flight?"

"Not really. As I said, it was a routine mission. We rarely have mechanical failures like what happened with Anosova's bomber, and never with a sudden altitude loss, especially with Callisto's weak atmosphere."

"No, I meant with Anosova."

Haralson hefted the bag of seeds as if they contained the answer. "She was her usual bitchy self. No offense. She was just, well, a PITA, if you know what I mean. Her crew hated her, and I had to correct her sorry-ass attitude a number of times. If you look at her record, you'll see the administrative actions taken against her by me. Hell, she was just short of an Article 15."

I scribbled on my digipad, but the notes were useless. I had already read over Anosova's information file and the documentation regarding Haralson's disciplinary actions. The way he crafted his notes, it was as if he had something personal against her. The same surfaced now, in his ruthless tone. Another hater like Captain Troy. So far, my impression of the crew of the spacecraft carrier was low.

"What about problems with the others aboard her craft? The audio on the cockpit voice and data recorder from the crashed bomber held a minute of arguing between Anosova, her copilot, Lieutenant Mendoza, and her crew chief, Sergeant Higgins. Have you heard it?"

"No. It was off-limits, pending investigation."

"Where were you during the incident?"

"I was in mission control with my NCOIC and the rest of my team. We didn't know what happened until after the crash occurred. They struck the outer ridge of the Valhalla crater within seconds of descent."

"I'm going to play the last two minutes of audio from the cockpit voice and data recorder. I want your take."

I pressed play on my digipad. The recording started with a loud drone in the background, followed by Mendoza asking Anosova what was wrong, and a shrill response by her in Russian, which my translation software displayed on-screen as a string of expletives. Anosova switched to English, accusing Mendoza of being an asshole, before getting cut short by Higgins, who yelled about the sudden loss of engine power. The drone intensified, making the exchange unintelligible, even for my translation software. It ended seconds later with Mendoza yelling, *What are you doing?* before the recording turned to static.

"What do you think?"

"It sounds like the loss of engine power surprised them too. It corroborates Engineering's assessment that the crash was due to mechanical failure."

"How about the argument between Anosova and Mendoza?"

Haralson didn't seem fazed by it. He sat back in his chair, unsympathetic. "As I said, no one liked her. It could have been anything."

"But this was personal. It had to be *something*. You heard Mendoza at the end. He was asking her, 'What are you doing?' right before the crash."

"You're assuming he was asking *her* the question."

I tapped the table with my nail. As much as I disliked Haralson's emotional detachment from the situation, he was right: Mendoza could have been asking Higgins the question, and it could have meant anything.

"So, what's your take on what went down?"

Haralson set his bag of seeds by his cup. "My take is the cause was catastrophic engine failure."

"You don't think this was an intentional act of sabotage? You don't think Anosova crashed her bomber on purpose?"

"No. And if she did, my team knew nothing about it. Now, if you don't mind, I've got some actual work to do."

I looked up at Lee, who shrugged.

"Thank you for your time, Commander."

.

*** END OF SNEAK PEAK ***

.

Thank you for previewing this military science fiction epic adventure. It's sold as its own eBook (https://tinyurl.com/ColdAsSpace) as well as part of the SPACE & TIME story collection in print and eBook format. Head over to https://www.stevepantazis.com/books or scan the following QR Code for your copy today.

About the Author

STEVE PANTAZIS is an award-winning author of fantasy and science fiction. He won the prestigious Writers of the Future award and has gone on to publish a number of short stories in leading SF&F anthologies and magazines, including *Nature, Galaxy's Edge,* and *IGMS.* When not writing (a rare occasion!), Steve creates extraordinary cuisine, exercises with vigor, and shares marvelous adventures with the love of his life. Originally from the Big Apple, he now calls Southern California home. You can learn more about him at https://www.St evePantazis.com.

Also by Steve Pantazis

Visit **https://www.stevepantazis.com/books** to see Steve's current and forthcoming releases or scan the following QR code.

Short stories and novellas:

A Matter of Time

A World Without Flowers

Aliens Anonymous

Apostate

Before I Let You Go

Between a Rock and a Fireball

C'est la vie, Humans

Chameleon

Cold as Space

Curse of the Goddess of Kaanapali

Cursed Magic

Daddy's Girl

Daughter of Time

Decadent Deception

Earth for Sale (Sold!)

Eternity's Traveler

Gods of War

Hex

Honor Bound

Humanity's Last Hope

I Dream of Stars

Illusions

In a Blink

In Darkness Lies

Infernally Yours

It's Only Skin Deep, Darling

Light in the Shadow of Worlds

Magic in the Land of Oppression

Murder on Moonbase 9

Odin's Daughter

Out of Print

Race to the Relic

Purple Orchid Eater

Reset

Surrogate

Switch

The Abernacle

The Daughter You've Always Wanted

The Devil Walks into a Bar

The Hunt

The Legacy

The Longest Mile

The Old Man and the Sea Siren

The Prize
The Sacrifice
To Be Human
Universal Problem
Unlucky
Untamed

Boxed Sets

Alien Worlds
Dragons & Magic
Human 2.0
Miscreants & Mayhem
Modern Magic
Robot Dreams
Space & Time
The Alien Within

Connect with Steve

Get a **FREE eBook** just by signing up for Steve's newsletter: https://www.stevepantazis.com/join

Support Steve at **Patreon** and receive early access to his short stories and novel chapters, along with cool swag: https://www.patreon.com/StevePantazis

To find out more about Steve and his happenings, check out these links:

Facebook page: http://facebook.com/SFFAuthor
Twitter: https://twitter.com/pantazis
Website: https://www.stevepantazis.com